THE STEEP ASCENT

THE
STEEP ASCENT

By Anne Morrow Lindbergh

Harcourt, Brace and Company, New York

A WARTIME BOOK

*This complete edition is produced in full
compliance with the government's regulations for conserving paper and other
essential materials.*

PREFACE

IT may seem an anachronism to publish today a flying story that is not a war story. The adventures of peace should not and cannot be set up against the adventures of war. But the writer must give out of his own store—which is in the past—and try by piercing deeply enough into his own experience, whatever it may be, to create something that is neither dated in time nor localized in space. I have tried to put into this story written at the end of a decade of flying (written in fact for the most part before the war) everything that those ten years taught me, as though it were a final testament. I have written under the constant realization—how could one help but realize—that the men who are fighting and dying in planes today are learning, in a few hours perhaps, what my years taught me slowly and with difficulty.

My experiences are not their experiences, nor my vision their vision. When they do speak, the aviators of the present war, what they say is usually far clearer than what earth-bound civilians can say. They seem, perhaps because of living more generously and fully in the moment, to have achieved a new sense of time and space, a new vision of the world, like the physical vision of that English Airman returning from a flight over the Mediterranean who looked back over his shoulder and "saw Crete like a pebble in a puddle, and all the blue mountains of Lebanon beyond."

Before that vision they are creating at such sacrifice one can only stand in homage—in homage to the vision and in homage to the sacrifice. One can only wait for what they have to say.

But in the meantime there are in the world today not only men fighting in planes but women behind them, if not literally then figuratively, in the back cockpits. Women who love and watch and wait eternally. My story is for them. Not only is it for them, it is about them.

For this story is fiction and not biography. Or, to be more accurate, it is a fictional account of an actual incident. It is not primarily an adventure story, at least certainly not one of physical adventure. And only in the most accidental and superficial sense can it even be called a flying story. Fundamentally it is simply a woman's story, the story of a woman's life and ordeal—any woman and any ordeal.

I have set the ordeal and the woman in the world of flying because the world of flying provides in a most compact and tangible form that "exceptional circumstance" of which Koestler speaks in his article on Richard Hillary. That exceptional circumstance which permits one to realize the intersection line of two planes of existence. Koestler, in his brilliant analysis of the well springs of creative writing, defines these two planes of existence as the "vie triviale" and the "vie tragique." "Usually," he states, "we move on the plane of the vie triviale, but occasionally in moments of elation, danger, etc., we find ourselves transferred to the plane of the vie tragique, with its un-common-sense cosmic perspective.

. . . But it happens that in exceptional circumstances —for instance, if one has to live through a long stretch of time in physical danger, one is placed as it were on the intersection line of the two planes."

This intersection line of the two planes would seem to me to be that same "point of intersection of the timeless with time" of which Eliot speaks in his long poem, "The Dry Salvages." Eliot says, I think rightly, that only the saint can apprehend the point of intersection of the timeless with time. But surely that point is the ceaseless preoccupation of all artists, and more consciously so in modern times. Is it not the preoccupation of Proust in his turreted edifice set up in the path of time; of Virginia Woolf in her recurrent *Waves;* of Kafka in his shadowy *Castle,* hovering over a village whose every paving stone is real and painful to the foot; of Rilke and his earth-hungry Angels; and of countless others who are trying with more or less success to achieve this precipitous point? The great Russian novelists have perhaps come the nearest to reaching it. They seem able with an incredible intensity to embrace the near and the far at the same instant, to synthesize the concrete and the abstract, the factual and the spiritual, the superficial and the profound. One of Dostoyevsky's heroes on the brink of suicide wants to live because of "the sticky little leaves of spring" . . . and "some great deeds done by men."

A writer's achievement would seem to me to be in proportion to his power to synthesize Koestler's "two planes of existence," or to reach Eliot's "intersection point of the timeless with time." To try—even if haltingly—to define or to translate that point into tangible form is, I believe, the artist's eternal task, and my own in this little story. Even though, as Eliot says in his beautiful poem, for most of us there are only hints and guesses, "hints followed by guesses."

> For most of us, there is only the unattended
> Moment, the moment in and out of time,
> The distraction fit, lost in a shaft of sunlight,
> The wild thyme unseen, or the winter lightening
> Or the waterfall, or music heard so deeply
> That it is not heard at all, but you are the music
> While the music lasts. . . .
>
> For most of us, this is the aim
> Never here to be realized,
> Who are only undefeated
> Because we have gone on trying—

The quotation of Arthur Koestler in the Preface comes from an article on Richard Hillary called "The Birth of a Myth," which appeared in the April number of *Horizon*, Vol. VII, No. 40, 1943. The lines of T. S. Eliot are part of his long poem, "The Dry Salvages," one of the four poems which make up his *Four Quartets*. The two verses quoted in Chapter V and again in Chapter VII are from a poem written by Patrick Shaw-Stewart in 1916 and published in an anthology of Maurice Baring entitled, *Have You Anything to Declare?*

CONTENTS

THE STEEP ASCENT

I

GOOD-BYE

SIX o'clock, Eve thought, looking at her wrist-watch. Time to say good night to Peter. The last time for weeks—for months perhaps. Six o'clock—where would she be tomorrow night at this hour? Somewhere on their journey. She did not know where. She only knew she would be looking back at this moment, this precise, ordinary and incredibly precious moment of saying good night to her boy. For weeks, for months now, she would be remembering. And it was still ahead of her. The anguish and the joy of that good night was still hers—but it was six o'clock. She could put it off no longer. She pushed open the heavy oak door that separated them.

"Are you in bed, Peter?" she said, stepping into his room. It was hardly a room, a tiny raftered hall of their old English farmhouse. "His Master's dressing room," the English caretaker had called it that day, so long ago, when he introduced his American mistress to it, breaking her in, Eve had thought a little wryly, to what an Englishman's wife should know. But it did for Peter now, tucked up into his four-poster bed, with kindergarten paper chains tacked to all the rafters and faded green curtains at the low leaded windows.

3

The small boy sat up and eyed her suspiciously. She had on her "London Clothes."

"I've come to say good night, Peter," his mother said with forced casualness. She said good night and not good-bye, because she wanted to make the last night just like every other one. She wanted to remember it that way. Now that she was losing it, the daily routine wore an extra bloom of beauty. Each trivial act they shared that day; their afternoon walk in rubber boots across the wet fields; their tea on footstools in front of the fire; their read during supper out of the interminable Peter Rabbit book:—all had been luminous with a last-time light. What a terrible burden it was, once the eyes were opened to it, this sense of the value of life, even ordinary life. She hoped her son would not inherit it from her. Perhaps if she were casual enough—

"I'm rather late," she went on evenly, "because—"

The boy was not deceived by the tone of her voice. He looked at her with stern gray eyes under a shock of untidy sand-colored hair.

"Where are you going?" he interrupted her coldly. There it was. She wished he were not so impressionable. He had all her American intensity combined with the sensitivity of his English father. Perhaps he would outgrow it. He was only five. She would like to protect him if she could from *Good-bye* and what it meant to her. All good-byes—what a wrenching they were, what a tearing of the limpet from its rock, and how weakening, as if one's life-force drained away at the word. Even ordinary good-byes were bad enough, after a week-end or on the station platform. But they were just dress rehearsals for the real kind. The real kind were those that implied "I may not see you again" or "I may not come back," "Life is uncertain," "One never knows." You didn't say that, of course, but it lay behind the word. It was the good-bye men said going to war; the good-bye you said to your husband when you went to the hospital to have a child, or the good-bye she said like this, going off on a flying trip with Gerald. Of course, it wasn't really so dangerous. Flying didn't have to be dangerous but— "One never knows." This time it seemed worse than before because of the child—the child she was expecting. That "good-bye" lay in her too. She wasn't really nervous; bearing a child was a normal process. Why not go off on the trip? But— "Life is uncertain." And Peter seemed to sense it already.

"You know, Peter," she said calmly, sitting down on the edge of his bed, "I told you I was going off on a flying trip with your father—to Egypt."

"*Tonight,* you're going?" He looked startled. She felt she had struck him unprepared in spite of all the packing going on in their room next door. He was too vulnerable sitting there, safe in bed in his night clothes. It would have been better, she thought vaguely, if she had said good-bye when he was protected by his outdoor clothes.

"Well, not tonight to Egypt," she smiled at him. "But we're going to spend the night in an inn near the airdrome to get an early start in the morning. And tomorrow we'll fly over the house, and you will wave out the window with a big towel the way you always do—"

It helped to say "the way you always do." It spread the misery of the present into the past and into the future. Thinned out like that, it was easier to bear. It assumed, too, that there would be a future. What happened "always" was secure as the seasons.

"When will you be back?" insisted the boy doggedly.

"Let's see," she said practically, "this is the end of January. February, March—" She counted on her fingers. "We ought to be back the first of April." (Only a month before the baby came— Yes, she'd have to be back by then.) "We'll surely be back by April. April is a wonderful month, Peter." Her mind rushed with relief over the chasms of the winter. "The yellow crocuses we planted around the quince tree will be out and the hyacinths coming up and—"

"Why do you have to go?" her son interrupted.

"Well—" She sighed. There was no use acting a part in front of your child. They always knew. Why was she going?—Why, indeed, if it was such a wrench? "Mother hasn't been very well," she said lamely, "she's been in bed, you know, and she has to go where it's sunny, and Father has business for the company in Egypt."

The boy was looking straight ahead as though he weren't listening to her. Oh dear, she thought, now he was going into that dream world he had, with all those imaginary people.

"Dandeleeshia has been to Egypt," he remarked gravely.

"I don't believe he ever sent you a postcard though, did he?" parried his mother lightly. She didn't know how to treat Dandeleeshia except to make slight fun of him.

"I'll send you postcards," went on his mother. "I'll send you a postcard of the Sphinx."

"What's the Sphinx?" said Peter, beginning to show more interest.

"It's—it's an enormous kind of lion in the middle of the desert."

"A *real* lion?" said Peter, his eyes fastening curiously on her now. She had certainly brought him back from Dandeleeshia.

"No, no,—not a real lion," she laughed, "a big stone lion."

"Like the lions at Trafalgar Square?"

"Yes, sort of—only much, much bigger."

"Was it always a stone lion," asked her son reflectively—"or was it once a real lion that got turned to stone?"

"Oh no—" she said emphatically, "it was *always* stone. It was made out of great blocks of stone—huge blocks—bigger than the coal-shed. And it took hundreds and hundreds of men and horses to move them. And then men carved them with huge hammers and tools, to make it look like a lion. It took years and years."

"Oh," he said, lying back on his pillow.

"Now good night, Peter," she leaned down to kiss him, letting her hand touch the top of his head lightly, to engrave in her fingers' memory the rough quality of his tumbled hair.

He was quite still now, staring up at the rafters. It was a good thing she remembered the postcards and the Sphinx, she thought. She could slip away on that. She jiggled back the green curtains and pushed out the creaking casement window into the damp night air. (Out into *that* they were going—the dark, the cold, the strange!) She drew back with relief into the human warmth of the small untidy garret-like room, with its single bare electric bulb braving the shadows, and her boy tucked up safely in bed under its protective glow.

"Well— Good night," she said again, reluctantly reaching the door and snapping off the vision from before her eyes.

"Mother?" called a voice from the dark. But the tone was calm now and reserved—even a trifle menacing, Eve felt.

"Yes, Peter?" She hoped he was not going to call her back again.

"Yes—?" she forced herself to say again drily, for there was an ominous silence.

"Dandeleeshia—" The words floated back slowly and impressively. *"Dandeleeshia* has a stone lion that was once a *real* lion."

"Oh," she said flatly, fumbling for the wooden latch on the old door. "All right" (falling back with some relief on the old-fashioned snuffer all mothers use). "Go to sleep now, Peter."

There was no use struggling against Dandeleeshia

tonight, Eve thought wearily. She had too much else to cope with. It would be different when there was another child. Peter would not be so much alone. It would not be so hard to leave him. Never, never again would good-bye be so dreadful—never.

II

DUST OF CONFUSION

EVE opened the door into her own lighted room. It was in frightful confusion. Boots, bags, sun-helmets, tools, tissue paper, coats, shirts, socks, and small bottles of drugs lay littered over the floor, the bed and the chairs. Her husband sat in the middle of the room, his crisp curls bent over a card table that was covered with maps. He had the end of a cigarette in his mouth and the ceiling was cloudy with accumulated smoke, a confused and misty mirror to the floor.

No wonder, she thought with dismay, that dogs crawled off in misery under beds when there was any packing going on. It was a complete upheaval of the order and security of daily life. She felt like crawling under the bed herself.

Nor could she notice any progress had been made in the packing since she left the room.

"Gerald," she said, winding her way delicately across the uncovered patches of the floor. "Gerald!" (For he had not yet looked up.) She hesitated, "Are we going to leave tonight?"

"In a jiffy, yes," he answered her, with his finger on a point on the map.

"Are you packed?" she prodded, standing ankle-deep in debris.

"Almost," he said, still not looking up.

"Do you want me to pack for you?" She insisted finally. She hated pinning him down that way but really—they would never get off and they would have to get a good night's sleep if—

"Would you mind holding the rule for me, darling?" He looked up at her at last through the clouds of smoke. "I can't seem to make a straight line."

"Maybe if you put your cigarette out," she suggested crisply. (After all, he would only drop the ashes on the map and burn a hole in it, and then out over Europe somewhere he would look and look for that vital town between two railroad tracks.)

"Possibly," he admitted drily, putting down the cigarette in an already full ash-tray.

"Are we going *right* over the Alps?" she asked, startled, looking down at the end of the rule she was holding.

"I was, yes, if the weather's good enough— Why not?" he asked, his pencil following the side of the rule.

"I don't know," she faltered. "It's—it's winter time."

"Quite, but we're not going to walk the blame things," he laughed.

"No," she giggled involuntarily. (It was odd enough to think of flying the Alps at this point but the picture of herself walking them—! With snowshoes, she mused, and—yes—a large Saint Bernard coming to the rescue with a tin of chocolate tied around his shaggy neck and—)

"At least, I hope not," added her husband. "There are passes, you know, and we can follow the regular air-route through them. I'm only trying to decipher the fortified zones. They've got Italy so boxed up now."

"Gerald," she said suddenly. "Do you think you'll be all right in Italy? The Ethiopian affair was only a year ago and they were stoning Englishmen in Rome then."

"I'll be all right." He waved off her worry with a careless sweep of his hand. "Though"—he stopped smiling now—"we'll have to settle that affair some day. We'll have to show them—"

The point of the pencil snapped off somewhere in Switzerland.

War. Eve didn't think she could face that tonight either, though it seemed to be always there, behind every word one said, like the glow of a distant fire throwing even small things into fantastic relief. She slid quickly to her next question.

"How far do you expect to go tomorrow?"

"Oh, I don't know," Gerald answered her. "We'll see." His speech was gay and staccato. "Can't tell without knowing the weather. If we had good weather we might get to Pisa. With a tail-wind"—he was becoming enthusiastic—"we might even get to Rome."

Eve took a side glance at her husband. His hair was as rumpled as Peter's and his cheeks ruddy. How *did* an Englishman's cheeks get so ruddy? It certainly wasn't from sunshine; it must be port and roast-beef. Though it wasn't that tonight. It was simply the trip. He just got drunk over trips, she thought ruefully, and it was she who had to fasten him down to facts.

She sighed. "Gerald," she started reluctantly, "you

will be careful, won't you? No long trips, no forced landings, no hair-raising escapes this time—"

"*This* time?" He looked up at her quizzically, his eyes crinkled up at the corners.

"I haven't been so hard on you, have I? I've never got you into any serious trouble."

"Gerald" (At times, the perpetual understatement of the English drove her crazy.), "what *is* 'serious trouble'?"

" 'Serious trouble' is—" He shook another cigarette out of his leather case.

"A crash no one walks away from?" she finished baldly for him.

"Quite."

"Well, I don't want any serious trouble." She felt she had to say it all now. "I don't want even mild trouble or the faintest mist of trouble on the horizon. I hate to keep bringing it up, but when you're carrying a child you just can't do the same things. A parachute jump or a forced landing—we'd both be dead—and even very bad weather—you get tense and if you get tense you get ill and—"

"Darling—" He put down his match, sobered at last. "I'll take care of you. No parachutes—no forced landings—no bad weather—I promise. That's why I'm taking you to Egypt because you've been ill. It's this beastly climate that's killing you." He paused for a moment and then pushed the maps away from him in an abrupt gesture. "But if you don't want to go—" He looked up at her gently and seriously. "If you don't feel well—" He looked worried now and appealing, like a child. "You *are* all right, aren't you, Evie? If you don't feel well I could go alone—or we could put it off a fortnight."

"Heavens, no!" she ejaculated. "Of course I'm all right." Put it off—she thought with a rush of exasperation—and go through all this over again? Good-bye to Peter and the packing and all the doubts? Heavens, no. Besides, in sober honesty, how would she feel if Gerald should suddenly change his nature? If he should rise up to his full height and say in fatherly fashion, "Now, my girl, you stay right here, safe at home with the chick. That's your place." Why—all the delicate structure of their marriage would tumble, like those glasses that are shattered, without a human hand touching them, by a single note ringing at precisely the right vibration.

"Of course I'm all right, Gerald." She protested again. "Really I want to go."

The warmth of her voice seemed to convince him.

"All right then." His face cleared like an open sky. "This is all done." He pushed back the table. "I'll finish the duffle bag, if you put in my clothes. Then I'll get out the car."

Eve started packing in earnest. The worst part of packing, she thought, sorting out the piles, is mental. Choice. The physical part was easy. All decisions were dreadful. Shall I—shan't I? Will I—won't I? No wonder Gerald let her do his. How cold would it be in Italy? How hot would it be in Egypt? Would they need quinine? And how about that Mother's Aid book, should she take it or not? No, she decided, definitely no. It was only full of academic advice that could not help her, like "Avoid all stress and strain" and "The expectant mother should not travel." She'd better forget about that. After all, she had made her decision.

In twenty minutes Gerald had taken both bags downstairs and had gone for the car. She was left to tidy up. The room was still strewn with abandoned choices. With a closed mind and haste at her heart, she stuffed them helter-skelter into drawers—any drawers—to get them out of the way. The room must be left in a semblance of order. Finally it was done. She turned at the door and surveyed it with a last look. It was cleared, true, but somehow it did not give the impression of order. All the big paraphernalia of packing had been removed from view: bags, tissue paper, clothes. But there was a fine dust of confusion left over everything. The shreds and scraps of packing had sifted everywhere as though a high wind had passed through the room and had just settled down. Well, she couldn't stop now to pick up each shred of cotton wool, each torn scrap of newspaper. It would take a long time before the room looked normal again.

She started down the stairs, her coat on one arm, carefully holding onto the bannister with the other. As a child she had watched her grandmother walking downstairs like this. What a waste of bannisters to hold onto them, she always thought then, when obviously they were made for sliding. But she couldn't slide now. She smiled as she remembered her grandmother, carefully feeling her way down the stairs with these same gestures. Pregnancy was like old age, she reflected; and waiting for birth was like waiting for death. It was inevitable but unpredictable. It was common as earth and magnificent as sky. And though it happened to everyone you had to go through it stark alone.

The great oak door was open into the hall below, the two bags, draped with macintoshes, standing beside it. She stepped out into the damp. Raining again! It always rained when they left on a trip, she thought gloomily. And there opened in her mind a long corridor of lugubrious leave-takings under umbrellas—drip-drip-drip. Never mind—perhaps it would be clear by morning. She stepped out into the wet. No rubbers or umbrella. After all, it seemed a little silly to start off with rubbers and umbrellas on a flying trip. The birds didn't use them. Careful of the stepping stones, now. They were always slippery in England; a kind of invisible moss seemed to grow on them. It would never do to fall here—remember the baby. Though why she should worry about crossing a stepping stone she did not know. After all, she thought recklessly, she was hurling herself over the Alps in less than twenty-four hours.

She settled herself in the front seat of the car while Gerald went back for the bags. The rain was running down the windshield and the headlights threw a misty glow ahead of her. Suddenly she remembered the cigarettes. Had Gerald put the last one out? Or was it still smoking up there in the room? It would fall off the tray, burn through the table and set the house on fire. The old beams would go like a haycock. Now really, Eve, she said firmly to herself, this kind of worry is a luxury. You won't be able to indulge in it tomorrow night. No, *but tonight.*

She slid out of the car and started back hastily along the stepping stones. Feet definitely wet now. Up the old stairs and into her door. She turned on the light. The room still had the air of a high wind in repose. The crumpled pile of dirty cigarettes was quite dead, although, coming in from the outside, the atmosphere was acrid from their smoke. She emptied the tray into the fireplace and started out again.

There was an unexpected scuffle under the bed. The dog, of course.

"Gubbio!" she said with a pang of remorse. She had forgotten all about him. "Oh, Gubbio!"

With great scratching of the carpet and thumping of his back feet, the big police dog dragged himself out from his hiding place. She had called him Gubbio after the wolf St. Francis tamed. He looked so fierce and he was so sentimental. The peaked black markings around his eyes and his heavy jowls always made him appear very mournful, but tonight he seemed more so than ever. His head drooped, just as though he had done something bad.

"Gubbio," she said, cupping her hand over the curve of his silky head and scratching the back of his flattened ears, "I am so sorry you can't go. Be a good dog, won't you."

He did not raise his head and made no effort to follow her to the door. He simply stood there, his body humped slightly in the middle, his tail between his legs, and his pointed head stretched out a little in her direction. Only his mournful brown eyes followed her as she turned to the door, and hungrily clung to the last flick of her feathered hat as she disappeared down the stairs.

Poor Gubbio, she thought, feeling her way down the bannister again. For a dog, good-byes were always the real kind.

III

THE HOUND OF TIME

SHE woke to the alarm clock, stabbed stark awake by its brazen insistence in the cold dark of early morning.

Yes—it is true! shouted the brutal bell rattling away on the dresser. *It is true—it is time. There is not a moment to waste.*

But why—why? she felt numbly, turning over in the unfamiliar hotel bed. *Say it isn't true!*

It is true—it is true—it is time, went on the alarm heartlessly, *not a moment to waste.*

Hush, you'll wake up the whole inn. She felt for it angrily and snapped it off. But yes, it was true. She remembered now. It was time—time to get up—flying—the Alps. They must be over the Alps by dark. Not a moment to waste.

"Gerald," she said, shaking him, "it is time. Time to get up." How anyone managed to sleep through that death rattle she could not see. "We must be over the Alps by dark."

And to be over the Alps by dark, her mind raced ahead as she pulled on her heavy wool stockings, they must get to the customs at nine—not open any earlier —and to get to the customs at nine, they must leave the hangar by eight; to leave the hangar by eight—

"Gerald, do hurry!"

She dressed with a terrible urgency eating at her.
Time was precious. Time, which had spread out for
her, as she lay in bed all winter, like an endless ocean of
identical waves—an ocean of nine months to be crossed
slowly with painful difficulty—time had suddenly tele-
scoped. It boxed them up. It was no longer infinite
space; it was a tunnel down which they were hurrying
on all fours, because there was no room to stand erect.
Time had been a slow mule she had prodded along to
keep it from going to sleep. Now it was harrying them,
snapping at their heels like a dog. Time had been a
blind man tapping down the walk after her. Now it was
a fencer parrying with them. Quick, quick, quick—
counter his thrust. Again—there he is again. Touché?
No, not yet—not yet, but—

"Oh, hurry, Gerald."

They sat in the darkened, blind-pulled dining room,
looking at dusty hunting prints on the walls. The
hounds in full cry, the scarlet coats, the leaping horses
were all frozen in mid-air over the country fence. How
leisurely they looked, how dead asleep under their
dust. But the haste of a hound was not the haste of a
stag, of a hare, Eve thought. She knew what it was, the
haste of a stag, of a hare; she felt it. She could hardly
drink her coffee or eat the soggy toast. There was something there at her throat that caught her breath. Time,
she thought; the hound of time had her by the throat.

And Gerald was so casual. Why was he so casual?
Paying the bill, putting the bags in the car—he even

went five minutes off their road to show her a modern house on the way to the airport.

"But I thought you liked to see modern houses. It's really a first-class one. It fits right into the landscape," he explained, astonished.

"Of course, of course, Gerald, I do," she began, "only it takes time. I'm afraid we'll be late. I can't see anything this morning—I can't think of anything until we get to the airdrome. You don't seem to remember—" she added in exasperation.

"I remember, of course I remember," he soothed her, "but we've got plenty of time and it's only five minutes."

Only five minutes! But time was made up of five minutes's. She felt about five minutes as her Puritan aunt used to feel about a stray pin gleaming on the floor. She could never "leave it lay." "Find a pin and pick it up—all the day you'll have good luck. Find a pin and leave it lay—" Ah, that was different! Superstitious—that's what she was about five minutes. That lost five minutes would gleam maliciously in the bottom of her mind all day.

Gerald wasn't like that; he wasn't Puritan at all. He had a kind of recklessness about him. She rather liked that recklessness, but not today. Here he was at the hangar looking at the new Falcon when they ought to be in the air—on the way to the Alps.

Not until she got into her familiar back cockpit in their small low-wing plane did she begin to breathe more easily. The roar of the motor was like blood pounding back in her heart; the wind in her face satis-

fied in her a sensation like thirst. The quickening
rhythm of the wheels down the sodden field hummed
triumphantly in her ears. They were off—at last they
were off! A short take-off, for the tanks were not full.
They'd refuel at Lympne. That was why they should
get there ahead of time. She glanced at her watch—
eight-twelve, it was.

Only twelve minutes late. That wasn't really so bad
—now they were actually off. Five minutes lost on the
road, two or three looking at the new Falcon, and
then those inevitable last moment delays just before
starting. The hangar doors always stuck in their
grooves when you went to push them open. And in-
variably there were two planes that had to be wheeled
out of the way before you could get out your own.
Funny about time. Lost time was like a run in a stock-
ing. It always got worse.

But still, now they were actually started, she had
a feeling of peace, of time spread out like space beneath
them. Gerald pulled back the throttle to a cruising
position. She pushed up both sides of the sliding cockpit hatch, so they met in the middle over her head. The
sound of the motor dulled to a monotonous drone. The
wind ceased whipping her hair in her eyes. Eve relaxed
in the sudden stillness and warmth; she looked out
through the slightly yellowed plexiglass at the sky.
It was what Gerald called "a good sky." She smiled as
she thought of that phrase so characteristic of him.
That meant—she looked out with an experienced eye
of appraisal—it was overcast, rainy even, with just an
occasional patch of blue. You could tell at a glance it

wasn't going to clear up. It would be raw and blustery
with showers all day. But there was no fog; that was the
only thing that really concerned Gerald. As long as
there was no fog and they were off, she didn't mind
either. "Mustn't grumble" as Gerald would say.

She took out the small scale map of Europe from the
side pocket and looked at the earth beneath them.
Croyden and the sprawling outskirts of London were
a black eruption of dingy roofs on their left, spilling
out over the rolling green countryside. (Even in winter, England was green.) They would soon leave the
disease of cities behind. Here were the hump-backed
downs with their open chalkpits. Here the valleys began, the lovely weald of Kent with its little villages and
handkerchief fields tucked here and there. Here soon—
she thought of it with the expectation of a child who
has a birthday gift to unwrap—soon out of that rolling
panorama would emerge their own private and special
bit of land, familiar and warm, lighting up the landscape.

There was the field with the mushroom-shaped oak
in the center, and the worn path like a wrinkled thread
lying across it—the field that she and Peter had walked
across only yesterday. Could it have been just yesterday? She looked back upon it as upon childhood. It
was dwarfed by emotional distance as the tree below
her was dwarfed by physical distance.

She always found that field first from the air and
then— Yes, the house, its old tiled roof, its vine-covered
walls, its autumn-red brick court. Familiar as a worn
doorknob, it was, but strange in this new perspective,

like one's own handwriting seen backward on a blotter. One had to trace it with one's finger in order to translate it. Yes, that gray puff at the door was the big rosemary bush, and those geometric scrolls were the garden walks, and those ninepins set up in a row were the poplar trees, and that lopsided nickel was the pool.

Gerald banked the ship up on its wing and started to spiral over this tiny spot in the landscape. He was pinning his finger on it, she felt, so not to lose it in the great world.

And suddenly the doll's house below became alive: a tiny flash of white from a window under the roof; figures running out into the court; and there was something, a large spider it looked like, cartwheeling about the garden—Gubbio, of course, barking his head off, probably.

She pressed her forehead against the plexiglass in order to take it all in her glance. At last she was released from time, out of the tunnel. The fencer sheathed his blade, the hound let go her throat. There was life, all of her life below her: her house, with its gray wings open like arms to the south; her garden, with its smoky hedges methodically drawn in curves; her boy, a minute figure now, dancing about the court waving something white that was larger than himself; her dog, that black spider going round in circles. Though it was only a few seconds, she had no pain at the approaching parting as she had yesterday. Oh no, yesterday she had left her world behind. She had given it up. And here it was again below her, given back and placed in the palms of her hands—like a promise. In recapturing it she felt she was recapturing it for good. It would always be there—somewhere: Peter, forever dancing in the court with his white towel, and she forever with her forehead pressed against the window and Gerald with his hand forever taut upon the stick. It was all hers, all in her possession for that instant. A long, long instant—an instant escaped from time. Or was this what time was? This bird in space, this free air to breathe, this century of peace. Time was no hound at the throat, she realized suddenly. Ah, *she* was the hound. Time was free, ever-present, eternal, calm. For in spite of the tight spiral that sucked the blood from her head, she had—as in all the great moments of life—no sense of speed or urgency. She was able to taste all her life with full appreciation and with full consciousness in that precious instant. Her boy, her home, Gerald;—all that she could never synthesize in daily living was somehow synthesized here. She could hold it in her heart at the same moment. No tearing of the sinews, husband and child, stay and go, earth and heaven, mortality and eternity. What was time? Where had it gone? There was left only an outer shell she had up to now looked upon as time—a husk only. The husk of time split open and let fall one seed—one seed of eternity.

IV

TAKE-OFF

GERALD pulled the wing up and leveled out the plane. The blood stopped pounding in Eve's head. Her sight was clear again and her breath even. She could feel the ship rocking in a gesture of farewell, dipping from side to side. But she did not look back. Her vision was over. She must put it away and not dwell on it any more. You didn't go back on your visions exactly but you must never—she had decided long ago—try to stretch them out past their allotted time and space. It was like a love-letter. Never re-read a love-letter, or, in fact, any letter. It coagulated—almost immediately after being opened—like blood. But it had once been a living, pulsing stream. It had been true once and it was still true, relatively, embedded somewhere in the past. That was enough. After all, she had had her vision. Completely satisfied, she tucked it away and set to work, no longer rushed, competent now and businesslike.

A glance at her watch. Eight-thirty-five. Plenty of time. They would get there before nine. Next, some house cleaning in this tiny space that was to be her only home for the moment. She made sure the two halves of the hatch were securely fastened above her head. She wrote down the time on her map and tucked

26

it away into its case. Then, unsnapping the safety belt, she turned around in her seat, kneeling on the cushion, to look at the baggage compartment in the tail. She had a brown leather cushion in her seat this time instead of a parachute. They had decided against parachutes in the end. For one thing, they were heavy, twenty pounds each. Forty pounds was nothing to sniff at in a light plane that was already overloaded and tailheavy. Besides, as she had told Gerald, it would be fatal for her to jump. No parachutes this time. Anyway, Gerald had said, "With the flaps down I can land this ship almost anywhere as easily as you would land in a parachute." Feeling the cushion under her knees Eve hoped this was true. She missed the hard security of the parachute seat. One always knew that if the worst came to the worst there was still that life-line to safety. Facing the tail compartment, she felt with her hand into its lumpy darkness. Canteens, coats, bundles:—all seemed fairly snug. Here was the paper bag with the lunch she had put up the day before. Better have it handy, up here in the corner where she could reach back easily.

There, she turned around again and settled herself forward on the cushion, with the dual control stick between her legs, and Gerald's brown leather coat and helmet visible in segments in the cockpit in front of her. My, it was badly stained, she noticed. There were still wet grease stains on his helmet and shoulders. How about her? Yes, her leather gloves and the new rainproof suit were stained too. What was it? Here was another spot on her arm, and here a bit of gray grease still sticking to the cloth. She dabbed hastily with a paper handkerchief. Where did it come from? she wondered with irritation and a frustrated sense of order. Looking up at the sliding cockpit windows, she found that the grooves were uneven with these same lumps of grease, gray with accumulated grit—to have them slide easily, of course. Well, they'd certainly done a good job, she thought grimly. She'd be covered with it soon. Of course one always got filthy flying but it was irritating to start out that way. She took another paper handkerchief and wiped along the grooves carefully. The grease was gone but it would come back, she knew; it worked out slowly. Before long, she thought philosophically, she wouldn't notice these first spots at all. Like the first scratch on a pair of new leather shoes, or the first wrinkle on your face, you knew pretty soon there'd be so many you would get over minding.

Probably there was grease on her face, too? A disquieting thought. She couldn't reach her compact. It was in the pocket of her inner trousers. To pull herself out of that heavy flying suit inside the cockpit was a feat of acrobatics she wasn't yet ready for. She was not a big woman but when she tried to move around in the cockpit her elbows hit against the sides and her knees got entangled between the stick and the metal seat. Better stay where she was. What *did* she have in her flying suit pockets? She started exploring them, one by one, with a sense of adventure. In the right knee pocket, a can of emergency rations; in the left knee pocket, a small first-aid kit; in the right breast pocket, several large handkerchiefs and some cotton wool for her ears; in the left breast pocket, an extra pencil and some milk chocolate. She wouldn't need that Saint Bernard after all, she thought with some satisfaction; she was completely outfitted herself.

A change in the rhythm of the motor made her sit up and look out of her inner world. They were gliding down toward Lympne. Already! Everything was going well now. There was the field below them on the rolling upland—that long uneven rectangle of green pinned down neatly around the edges with boundary lights. Gerald opened his hatch for landing. The blast of the engine hit her ears squarely and the wind snapped her hair from under the helmet again. They began a leisurely circle over the field. She had plenty of time to look at the sheep meadow on the far slope, at the row of hangars (Not a plane in sight—it was Sunday morning.), at the line of small white frame offices, at the pine trees along the road. And, beyond, down the hillside, those rather grand houses with gardens and terraces and a view—yes, they must have it, for she could see it definitely now—a view of the Channel, the curve of gray water where the land met the sea. It was overcast. She couldn't see far, but still, it wasn't foggy. It was a "good sky," and they were on time; she was satisfied.

Eight-forty-nine— They touched the ground. The comfortable earth sound of bumping wheels replaced the roar of the motor. Eight-forty-nine— Plenty of time. They taxied up to the end hangar. No sign of life, but Gerald swung the ship around with a blast of the engine so it faced the big red fuel pump outside. A mechanic in blue uniform appeared around the corner of the hangar about the time they cut the switch. He sauntered over to the cockpit, giving a vague gesture of salute.

"Morning, Sir. Have your tanks filled up?"

Gerald pushed the flap of his helmet up off one ear. It gave him rather a rakish air.

"Right—both tanks, if you will. She'll take about seventy gallons. And—a—we're in a bit of a hurry to take off." He raised himself in the cockpit. "If you don't mind, we'll leave her here and just go over to the customs office to save time."

"Right you are, Sir."

Eve unsnapped her safety belt and followed her husband out of the plane. As they started off toward the line of white shacks the mechanic called after them:

"I'm afraid he isn't there yet, Sir."

"What!" They both stopped still and looked at him in astonishment. She never expected this, Eve thought naïvely. *They* might be late, but other people, *never.* It was unfair.

"But I thought they always opened at nine?"

"As a rule, yes," said the mechanic, not breaking the routine of his work and reaching for the hose. "He's almost always there by nine, but I haven't seen him yet this morning. Need any oil, Sir?"

"Better see; she might take a quart or so," said Gerald perfunctorily. And to the larger problem, "Well, we'll go and have a look at the office." They had nothing else to do and having started in that direction there seemed no real reason to stop. They had turned toward the road again, when the mechanic called after them, as an afterthought:

"He's had a spot of trouble with his car."

"Oh," said Gerald.

"A spot of trouble!" fumed Eve under her breath. The eternal English. Now what did *that* mean?

"How big is a spot, Gerald?"

"Well," he began drily, "can't say. It might mean he can't get it started, or it might mean he's run into the ditch. There are spots and spots." His eyes crinkled up at the corners as he looked at her. "For instance, you have two spots on your flying suit and one black smudge on your chin."

"I know," she said hastily, reaching for a handkerchief. (How unkind of Gerald!) "Flying," she said, in a burst of irritation, "is the slowest, dirtiest, and most unreliable form of transportation on earth."

"Yes," he said, throwing back his head and laughing at her. "But it's fun too."

"Sometimes," she admitted. This was not one of the times.

They peered through the window of the locked customs house, as though they might find some clue to today from the dead scraps of yesterday. But there were no scraps. There was no fire in the coal grate and the desk was neat and bare. There was no sign of a customs officer and no sight of a car on the road. They glanced down its uneven track as it led off past the pine trees at the end of the field. There was no use watching a road. It was like watching the mail for a letter.

Gerald turned on his heel in the quiet of a suddenly empty morning.

"I think I'll go over to the club," he said, "might be someone there. Want to come? You'd be more comfortable there," he added considerately.

"No—I'll stay here." She was comfortable enough where she was, encased in layers of flying clothes (for the Alps). And she didn't want to see *anyone*. One was awkward enough carrying a child, and in that flying suit —with a smudge on her chin! It really seemed superfluous of fate, that smudge. She didn't mind the other things. But it was definitely unsportsmanlike to give her a smudge.

"No, I'll stay here—besides, he might come any moment. Keep an eye out, won't you?" The club was dead anyway. And there was nothing so dead as a dead club, on a Sunday morning with the fires unlit, an empty bar, faded chintzes at the dark windows, and comic cartoons of crack-ups thumbtacked to the walls, and curling at the edges with age.

The hangar was dead on a Sunday morning too. But she preferred a dead hangar any time to a dead club. She walked slowly back in the direction of the plane. The hose was dangling from the first wing tank. She looked at her watch. Nine-ten. At any rate, the gas was still going in. That made her feel better. While the gas was still going in, time was not being wasted.

The mechanic nodded at her taciturnly as she came up. She found a kind of pleasure in the contact although she would have disliked seeing anyone at the club.

"Been any planes in this morning?" she asked.

"No, not yet. It's rather quiet here of a Sunday morning," he answered her. "But Imperial Airways took off only an hour ago—dropped down here last night—pretty thick, it was—couldn't get into Croyden." He shook his head mournfully. "Such a spell of weather we've had lately—never seen a January like it," he added with finality.

"Yes," she said, joining in his gloom with some warmth, "hasn't it been a wretched year!"

"What February will be like—can't say," he continued on the same note, moving the hose to the second tank. "Generally speaking, we have our worst weather in February. Nasty month, February."

"Horrible, isn't it," agreed Eve, leaning over to pick the mud off her boots with a little stick. What a nice man, she thought, as they relapsed into silent concurrence on the weather. She felt quite cheerful now, joined to the world of human beings again by this act of participation in gloom. Yes, she was feeling better every moment; but the moments were passing. Now that the gas was almost in, time was beginning to count, to waste away. The taximeter in her had started ticking again. Nine-twenty—where *was* that man? He must really be in the ditch, as Gerald said.

She sauntered around the corner into the murky hangar. There were three or four light biplanes dovetailed into one end, two with their engines out, and one wing leaning up against the wall, with the fabric off it. She started walking all around them, carefully ducking under wings and dodging propellers, pretending to look at them very carefully. Every now and then she would glance down the road. Still no car. Nine-thirty—it was hopeless then. In desperation she began to read day before yesterday's weather map on the wall, an academic pursuit only, since all those feathered wind arrows and distended circles of high and low pressure areas must have blown away by now. Then the printed notices, official orders and restrictions under the Lion and the Unicorn seal: "By order of his Majesty's Government." "His Majesty's Government has authorized . . ."

Nine-forty—he would never come. And she was getting tired of standing up. She could sit down on the wheel of that dolly over there, or lean against the tractor. But it would soon get cold. Where was Gerald? Sitting in the club drinking tea? That might be rather nice. They would just stay here all day, she decided, now reconciled to the idea, and then get a fresh start tomorrow morning. If the man didn't turn up by ten she'd go—

Oh heavenly day! Down the road was coming a baby Austin. Could she get to the office before him, she wondered breathlessly? Now, *where* was Gerald? She had not reached the road before she saw her husband coming down it from the opposite direction. They both arrived at the steps of the customs shack before the officer could get out of his car. He looked at them sheepishly, fumbling for the keys in his coat pocket.

"I'm most awfully sorry, Sir," he said with a soft Scotch burr in his voice. All Eve's resentment melted at once.

"Been having trouble with your car?" asked Gerald kindly.

"Yes—haven't been able to get it started these past mornings." The man had a slightly grieved look as though he were speaking about a child. ("It's his tonsils, Doctor. They always *have* bothered him.")

"They do get gummed up in the winter, sometimes," offered Gerald sympathetically. "We're in a bit of a hurry," he went on more briskly, "because . . ."

"I know—I know—" The officer slammed the door of his car. They followed him up the steps as he clinked the key in the lock, and stamped into the damp office after him, like impatient dogs at his heels.

The familiar customs forms came out of the drawers and were filled out quickly. Gerald made out the International Carnet.

No, they had no firearms, or camera to be sealed. Destination? Rome.

"Wouldn't you like the weather, Sir?"

"Oh, I don't believe we'll bother, thank you." Gerald never worried much about weather ahead as long as it was good enough to fly where he was. Besides, the morning was getting on. He started for the door. "We're rather anxious—"

"It's directly on your way, Sir—this second building—and—a—you owe me a penny, Sir—His Majesty's regulations—"

The weather man was chewing at his pipe as they stopped at the door, but he obligingly looked over his maps and reports. "You may find some clouds over the Channel—nothing very bad, though. France—let's see—

France is overcast—about 6000 feet. There's a layer of lower clouds too—some rain perhaps in Eastern France. Switzerland, about the same—"

"Won't the Alps be covered then?" insisted Eve suspiciously as they waited for something more concrete.

"Well," said the weather man, still chewing on his pipe, "can't tell, the Alps go up pretty high, you know. Their heads might be sticking up in the stuff."

The English! The English! Eve thought to herself, were they really as casual as all that or was it simply a pose?

And Gerald was just as bad. "We'll have a look at them anyway," he said amiably. "We can always go round. 'k you." And they were off.

At last, Eve felt, as the now heavily loaded plane lurched down the grass toward the far corner of the field. So they'd have to take off from the lower end— she glanced at the wind-sock on the hangar as they lumbered by and made some swift calculations in her mind. That meant taking off up the slope, with full tanks—and over those pine trees, too. That was bad. The field wasn't any too long, either. Gerald was pushing down to the very end. They couldn't afford to waste an inch of ground. He blew the tail around neatly in the corner. There was hardly a foot left between them and the fence. He set the brakes and lifted himself up in the cockpit, peering out over the engine-cowling at the field ahead of him.

Eve recognized this familiar gesture. He always covered the ground with a last perfunctory look before taking off. But this time the look was more than per-

functory. It was a long look of appraisal which not only
noted down details but also weighed them in some invisible scales of the mind. He was looking, Eve knew,
at that rising slope of green stubble, at the row of
hangars at the right, at the pointed pine trees dead
ahead on the sky line. What did they weigh against the
power of a motor, against the lift of the wings, against
the slight breeze that billowed the wind-sock? He was
thinking, she guessed, of that controllable pitch-propel-
ler they hadn't yet been able to buy. With a propeller
like that they could leap any hurdle—even the pines.
They could climb straight up the steepest stairs of air,
but this way—

Gerald settled back abruptly in his seat. He clicked
on his safety belt. He had decided, then. The invisible
scales had tipped toward them. He thought they could
make it. He pushed the throttle open and checked both
magnetos. The roar of the motor blocked off the outside world. Vibrations surged through the plane in a
gigantic current of power. It shook confidence into Eve
and she felt like bowing before it as to some mighty
pagan god. How could anything go wrong with such
a power on their side?

And yet, how slowly, once he released the brakes,
did they get away, almost as though the ship hesitated
before the approaching leap, like a horse balking at a
high jump. Slowly they gained momentum up the
stubble slope; slowly climbed. Surely it wasn't uphill
all the way? When would it level off? They were almost
halfway. They were even with the hangars. They were

over the slope now, but not going nearly fast enough to get off. They were still earth-bound.

There comes a moment in a take-off, long before the wheels leave the ground, when you know you are going to get off. It is as though at some indefinable point the plane shifts its allegiance from earth to sky. It may still be traveling along the earth's surface, apparently tied to it, but in reality it has severed its cord; it has acknowledged, secretly somewhere, that its element is air. Eve held her breath for that moment of acknowledgment, that shift in allegiance, but it had not come. No, they were still earth-tied, bound by earth's limitations, forced to obey her laws. Bump-bump-bump over the ground. And the pine trees sticking up ahead, growing taller every moment. This time they really weren't going to make it. Could they stop? Enough room? Jam on the brakes? Ground-loop, even? Why didn't he cut the throttle? Gerald was a brilliant flyer but— Oh God, oh God, not in those pine trees, not in the back yard of those big estates— No. Over the Alps, all right, God, but not here on Lympne airport.

Oh—they were off. Another bump. Yes, they were off. But the pines were ahead. He wasn't climbing fast enough. Eve's arms ached to pull back the stick, right back to her chest and make the plane leap into the air, like a salmon up a waterfall. That was crazy, of course. That's how flyers got killed. They'd just stall and fall off, right into the pines or the terraced gardens. Gerald knew the edge. He always played very near it, but he knew where it was, and they were on it now. Ah, he was turning slightly. He shouldn't do that either, but

he could. That was the edge; the trees were lower there
on the right. Yes, they'd make it now. They were gain-
ing on the trees. Now they were over them, just skim-
ming over their pointed tops. They were over the
ridge; the big valley opened out generously below
them. It was downhill all the way now, all the way to
the sea. My, but it was close that time, Eve breathed
with relief. It ought, she felt with a Puritan sense of
expiation, to earn them safe passage the rest of the
journey.

But the time? Eve glanced at her watch. An hour
late! Heavens, a whole hour. A great rent was torn
open in the unbroken bolt of their beautiful day. She
stared, incredulous, at the yawning gap. A whole hour—
it could never be mended. They would just have to get
on with the torn day as best they could. What a delicate
fabric it was— Time. How easily it got soiled or ripped.
A splinter here and a thorn there; an extra turn on the
road, a "spot of trouble with the car," a hangar door
that stuck—and the thing started going to pieces. How
vulnerable one was cloaked in such a garment, depend-
ent on it. No one knew, but those who wore it, how
vulnerable one was.

She looked down on the world below. They were
cruising over the estates on the hillside, peering down
impudently into their privacy: the swimming pool, the
terraced garden, the lines of poplar trees. There was
no sign of life—a Sunday morning. What were they
doing down there, those gentlemen of leisure? Taking
another kippered herring or another cup of tea? Reading about the tufted Titmouse in the nature notes of

the *Times?* Or even, perhaps, if they had been up late the night before, turning over in bed for another snooze, while she and Gerald, Eve thought with a sinking heart—she and Gerald had started out for the Alps —an hour late.

V

ACHILLES, O ACHILLES

THEY were climbing slowly for the Channel hop.
Gerald had not yet set the throttle for cruising.
The roar of the motor sang through the ship exult-
antly. It was the exultation of having just a little more
power than necessary. Eve felt it in her bones and ral-
lied to it. The ship felt it and seemed to leap into the
air like the salmon. They were banking, too, turning
slowly so that new things came into sight at each instant. The world shifted before their eyes—the world
of flying that Eve knew so well but which excited her
always as though it were being unrolled for the first
time.

Folkestone was ahead of them. She could see the
sharp cliff dropping down to that crowded collection of
drab roofs and chimney pots on the water's edge. She
could make out the harbor now, the tidy docks holding
the white channel boats in which they had crossed so
many times, slowly and painfully, over the endless
Channel. Toy boats they seemed today in a toy harbor
way below. "What is man, that thou art mindful of
him?" crossed her mind arrogantly as they left the toys
behind.

Under the billowing gray clouds further out she
could see the tugs and freighters coming in, bobbing

41

up and down on the choppy whitened waves of the gray Channel. Boats from all directions met here in converging lines, drawn to a single point, like iron filings drawn to a magnet—the magnet of England.

While she and Gerald were setting out! This was the joy of flying, Eve felt—to set out, especially in the morning. There was a freedom about it, a limitless feeling of space and time. The day and the world stretched before them, endless, like summer to a child (Fields and fields of buttercup-and-daisy summer.) or life to a youth (Night and their destination were as distant as death.). She felt full of joy. How right Gerald had been to go. All her fears and misgivings dropped away. The take-off was behind them, the day was ahead—and France.

She could not see France because of the low clouds, and those straight gray chiffon curtains of rain dropped down in places shutting off her view. But France was there, waiting for them, like the day.

The further off from England, the nearer 'tis to France—

The nursery rhyme bounced absurdly in her mind:

The further off from England, the nearer 'tis to France,
Will you, won't you, will you, won't you, will you join the
    dance?

I will, Eve thought, I will, for better or for worse, for richer or for poorer— How silly! It was the bouncy day that made her mind jump inconsequently. Rough air. She was glad of that. She preferred bouncy weather to smooth. She didn't like the air smooth as satin. She preferred it nubbly, like tweed. Otherwise you lost its texture, its consistency. And how she loved texture in all its forms.

In eating, for instance, so few people seemed to feel that way, but she always thought texture was almost more important than taste. That was what was wrong with English cooking—the texture, not the taste. There was no texture to those doughy dumplings or those limp, over-boiled Brussels sprouts. Take the texture of the crust of hard French bread for instance, or the texture of roasted chestnuts. (They mustn't be crumbly and they mustn't be rubbery—just right.) Or, best of all, the texture of a certain kind of mild runny Italian cheese. Not the cheese itself, but the slightly firmer rind with a little resistance to it. Just to think about sinking her teeth into it made her mouth water. And texture to one's fingers, too, tweed, yes, and home-spuns and wool. (All those modern shiny plastic ma-terials had no texture.) And certain kinds of heavy velvety paper in a book. And hair— She could close her eyes and still feel Peter's curls in the tips of her fin-gers. And the texture of snow, and leaves underneath the snow, that were frozen and crisp with frost and crunched deliciously under your feet. The joy, too, of walking over a newly plowed field, the texture of the clod giving way under your instep, when it was firm but not too dry. It must not pulverize into dust; it must have resistance enough to crumble into fine rich earth as your foot sank into it.

Oh, she was very earthy, Eve decided a little rue-fully. She loved this earth and earth things. She sank into her flying suit and felt warm and comfortable and slightly ashamed of her enjoyment. Gerald loved the sky but she loved the earth. She was an earth-child. And when she was above it like this, looking down on it from inside her rounded glass eggshell, she loved it even more. Was it distance only? Was it the fear of losing earth that made you love it so much? She always felt full of a terrible tenderness toward the earth when she was above it. Sometimes it was unbearable. She wanted to hold it in her arms and comfort it.

Here was France, now, the dim gray outline coming through the veils of rain. Cap Gris Nez raised its head out to sea. And there followed the long gentle line of the coast. Now—now they were over France; France was below them. France stretched ahead of them: the rolling fields, the wet roads marked with poplar trees—rows of them like the teeth of a comb sticking up on end—the little villages of tiled-roofed houses, who looked as though they had all been playing follow-the-leader round in a circle until they got stuck and never got unwound again. And the fields again, the rolling open fields.

How lovely France was—how she warmed to it as it spread out, how it lifted her heart. Why? Because it was not boxed up in hedges like England? Because it had an easy and untidy and out-of-bounds look, like America? No, she didn't think it was just that. It was simply France, the quality of France. Grace lay over it like the bloom on a ripe plum. Even the ugly parts of France had some of this grace, even the industrial north they were headed across now, even the flat stretches of the pine-treed southwestern coast. It wasn't its beauty, for it wasn't exactly beautiful. It was like a woman who is not beautiful but who has all the gestures of beauty. That was better than being beautiful; it was giving the impression of beauty. People always fell in love with a woman like that; and people fell in love with France.

It wasn't like England, now. Eve lifted her eyes from the fields of France and let them rest on Gerald's sturdy brown leather coat staring back at her from the front cockpit. England, people were always saying, was a garden. She hated them to say it. It was such an obvious statement, and yet it was true, in a way. She could remember her shock of delight at the incredible greenness of the English grass and trees that first spring, at the incredible vividness of the pink orchards and flowering bushes—spectacular beauty, garden beauty. You didn't fall in love with a garden, though, but with a field, like one of these fields in France, rolling up over the hill to somewhere you could not see. A field had some mystery to it, something hidden, whereas in a garden it was all there on the shelves. "Come look— Come look!" shouted a garden. "I'm here," said a field, simply; "I'm here."

But the real reason she objected to people saying that England was a garden was that they had missed the quality of England. England was a garden, yes; and beautiful. But the essential quality of England was not in her beauty. It was in something else, Eve always felt. It was in those tugs and freighters chugging their way across the choppy Channel; in the stumpy round oak trees in the middle of the fields. It was in the postmistress of their little valley who was old and had a bad knee but who ran the post office, counted the mail, took the telegrams, minded her son's baby, was grandmother to the whole community; and who, if there were a war, would probably be running all of the relief work in the valley—casually, you know, just as a matter of course.

It wasn't just courage—"Guts," as she would say in America—it was a kind of gallantry, and gallantry was more than courage. It was courage, Eve decided, plus something else, plus a carelessness of self. No, that was recklessness. What made the difference? Recklessness was blind, but gallantry had its eyes open. It was aware. That was what it was, and the English had that quality of aware generous courage. It was very Greek, too, she always thought, like those Greek epitaphs found on gravestones all through the Aegean world. They so often asked the traveler to give a thought to the soldier who died there—"far from home—" and sometimes, explaining his sacrifice, they would add that he "lost lovely youth facing the rough cloud of war." How English that was. They always knew what they were giving up when they went to war. "Lovely Youth"—"Far from home."

It wasn't so far from home at that. It was right here where they were, over France. Eve pressed her head against the plexiglass to look out at the slightly murky world below. They were going through the coal country. She could see, in the half-dusk of an overcast day, smoky peaks rising to smoky curtains of cloud. Here and there one could make out a blurred smudge, in the narrow field of vision, that was not rain but the smoke from the chimneys of some factory town. There were flooded patches in the treeless fields below her. A river—she glanced at the map—the Somme—Cambrai was just above her finger. Grim names. Yes, it was here. It was here, perhaps, that the officers went out into one of the early tank attacks, when there was no defense against those new and deadly monsters. Gerald had told her how they had walked out, in the full knowledge of immediate and certain death, twirling their riding crops as they went, only to be mowed down by machine guns. If that were not gallantry, what was?

"Lovely Youth"—"Far from Home." Yes, it was very Greek. No wonder that a British soldier had called on Achilles at Gallipoli. That poem found on the soldier killed in battle—Gerald had read it to her last winter as she lay in bed and she could not erase it from her mind.

> Was it so hard, Achilles,
> So very hard to die?
> Thou knowest and I know not—
> So much the happier I.
>
> I will go back this morning
> From Imbros over the sea;
> Stand in the trench, Achilles,
> Flame-capped, and shout for me.

Eve could hear his gentle English voice reading it. Gentle and cool, and yet he knew what it meant, as though he had written it himself. For he had that kind of gallantry—courageous and aware. She glanced at his

brown leather coat, wrinkled and worn just ahead of
her in the front cockpit. It was strange to be so close
to him—she could put out a hand and feel the rubbed-
off part of his coat at the shoulder blades; she could
see the squint wrinkles around his eyes as he half
turned to look at the compass between them; she could
touch his firm roughened hand as he pulled off his
leather gauntlet to adjust the knob; they were so close
in this tiny eggshell compartment hurling through
space—and yet, he did not know she was thinking of
him. The engine, roaring continuously, wove a spell
that separated them like sleep. She could break the
spell, of course; she could lean forward and touch his
shoulder and then— But no, she wouldn't, Eve decided,
she would sit back in her tiny world, with her map in
her mittens, and think only about him. She was warm
and sleepy. The day stretched ahead endless, and those
rain clouds, and France. The Alps were ahead of them
—but so far ahead. She had time to think out—what
was she thinking out? Gerald and his gallantry.

Yes, Gerald was gallant. He knew the edge and he
played it casually. She supposed that was why she had
fallen in love with him. For she had met him when he
was stunt flying at the Cleveland Air Races one year.
How she got there she never quite understood. Her
brother had asked her to be one of the hostesses for the
"Foreign" pilots—because she'd been abroad, she supposed, and spoke a little French, and was vaguely inter-
ested in aviation. She remembered the hot grandstands,
the dusty field, the pylons rising high out of the haze,
the crowds of people, and that strange mixed group,

standing around awkwardly in the "box," she was supposed to entertain.

She hadn't known who Gerald was. He didn't look
like an aviator. He was one of those lean angular Englishmen who bent over politely when he talked to her.
And his eyes were always crinkled up, with concentration or amusement—she couldn't make out which. She
remembered the tweed of his coat; it showed unusual
taste for an aviator, she thought, not having much
regard for aviators then. He didn't look all dressed up
to fly, in leather coat and boots. In fact, she had asked
him naïvely if he *did* fly. And he had said, "Yes—I fly"
—casually but with finality, one of those blinds-down
answers of the English. So she had changed the subject.
"Don't you think," she had said, feeling around for a
way out of her trouble, "we had better go over and
talk to that Frenchman? He looks rather lonely."

"Right!" he had said amiably, lifting up the window
blinds again, "I know the first few lines of the *Marseil-
laise!*" How she had laughed! They both laughed. (She
smiled still when she thought of it. Looking at his
leather coat in front of her—laugh wrinkles seemed to
crease the back of it.) After that there was a kind of
private pact between them. And then he had gone out
to fly. Someone had said to her carefully wrapped-up
question, "Didn't you know? That's Gerald Alcott—
he's the Schneider Cup racer and one of the most brilliant stunt flyers in the world—you wait and see."

So she had waited. But much to her horror he had
come out in a funny little biplane that looked pasted
together with adhesive tape. He had flown over the

field like a wobbly sparrow, not keeping a straight line like the other pilots, almost hitting the ground. She had been terrified, missing the fine points of his "flying-fool exhibition," and had only thought with surprising pain, "That nice young man has been drinking—I always heard pilots were wild—and he's going to get himself killed." Until someone behind her said, "Gosh —but he's good—did you ever see such grass-cutting!" Then she was a little annoyed at her concern. So that was it, grass-cutting! She apologized later at the party that night but he had only laughed and changed the subject. "How about that Frenchman," he had suggested tactfully, "hadn't we better go and look him up?" So they had gone off together, sharing their private pact.

How lovely it was—that private-pact sense, almost as nice as being all alone together in a tiny plane over the great strange world. Not, of course, that they ever found the Frenchman, she reflected, smiling. It really wasn't necessary.

And then, and then—Eve stirred stiffly in her bulky flying suit—after that, her life had kaleidoscoped so fast:—their marriage, the trip to England, and Peter. How could she have foreseen that her heart would get wound up in Peter? And their life in the valley, so calm and peaceful, only interrupted by those strange wild flying trips—it had slipped by with hardly a moment to stop and look at it, those eight, nine—my, was it ten years? When life was happy it went fast, like this swift flight over France. Eve liked the sense that a flight was going fast. It was more magical that way.

Where were they? She pressed her head against the window again.

The overcast had lifted a little. There was no more rain. Only the heavy layer of clouds darkened the earth beneath them. She looked down at the wet fields. What were those zigzag lines of lighter brown in the dark brown fields? Oh, she realized with a shock, the trenches, of course. How could she forget? This was the war country, and the trenches, although filled in and plowed over, were still a different color. Even after twenty years the earth had not forgiven. She stared down at those faint but unmistakable zigzag lines with a growing sense of nausea in the pit of her stomach.

> Stand in the trench, Achilles,
> Flame-capped, and shout for me.

It would take an Englishman to see Achilles in a trench. Gerald would see him, of course. But then, Eve thought grimly, if there were a war, Gerald would not be in a trench. He would be in the air. It was cleaner there. She could picture him better, while he *was* there —for it would not be long. They would all be killed off, the first crop—like those English officers walking against the tanks. And he would be in the first crop. Of course, she knew *some* men did survive a war, but not *hers,* she felt with a pessimistic lack of logic. Not Gerald. He was *too* gallant. She was almost angry about it. Even in peacetime, she thought, with a flicker of humor, he was sometimes a little too gallant.

Take that trip to Iceland, for instance— Gerald's impassive brown leather coat stared at her dutifully from

the front cockpit. Should she fly? Eve wondered with
vague feelings of compunction. Was it selfish of her
to go off alone like this in her thoughts? Like going
to sleep when the other person was tossing around
sleepless at night. She always resented Gerald's going
off peacefully to sleep when she was lying there stark
awake. But still—no—he didn't mind flying. He said
so; he did it instinctively. And it wasn't late, only
twelve o'clock. Later, she would fly—later. The day was
still young, still a lot of it left, like a pie. She had only
started to cut into it and hadn't yet begun to count
whether there would be enough pieces to go round.
Besides—falling back into that comfortable easy-chair
of excuses—she was having a baby. "The pregnant
woman should not over-tire herself. She should try to
relax." Relax, Eve.

Now, take that trip to Iceland. They had gone in
the Moth—much too small it was—with floats attached
to it. Gerald had wanted to go on to Greenland and
Canada but they had turned over in the bay at Reykjavik and almost got drowned. That was a close one.
Eve drew in her breath at the thought of the long
instant before the plane flopped over. The American
with the big expedition up there had fished them out.
She remembered so well, at first she had felt proud
of her countryman. (See, that's the way we are—generous, big-hearted!) But then later, as they all three sat
around talking it over at the hotel at night, she began
to feel irritated at him.

He had shot out practical questions at Gerald in his
curiously flat voice. "What speed does your plane

make?" "How much load does it carry?" "What range?"
Like sausages from a meat machine, those questions
chopped out. And then his *figures*—he kept laying
down figures as to the winds in Greenland. "Those
foehn winds come down the fiords like a bat out of
hell—more than a hundred miles an hour, some of
them. Don't you see if your Moth ran into one of those,
Alcott . . ." He had not pressed his point but it was
clear he thought they were attempting the impossible.
"Our statistics show," he went on seriously, "that the
mean weather in Greenland—" "Oh bother statistics!"
Gerald had said, flying off the handle completely at
that. And then, to make it worse, he added, flinging
down his gauntlet, "I don't believe in statistics." The
American would have been much less shocked if Gerald had said, "I don't believe in God." He was quite
unaware, Eve had realized helplessly at this point, that
Gerald had just sky-rocketed up into that lovely cloud-
cuckoo-land of British conversation which completely
baffles the poor foreigner. Left standing below on the
earth, he does not understand that the game has now
suddenly changed its locality. They are no longer box-
ing in the world of facts alone but bantering about in
the upper reaches of humor, fantasy, and philosophic
truth.

"Why reduce flying to a formula like that?" Gerald
had pursued, happily spinning away at his private
bowling game in the clouds.

"Because," the American had blurted out, still stum-
bling about on earth, "you're apt to get bumped off
if—"

"Oh well," Gerald had gone on, doing a series of conversational barrel-rolls, "you've got to take a few chances of getting killed." He was having a wonderful time, Eve remembered. She had begun to feel sorry for the American, then.

"Sure—sure," her countryman had stammered. "But, but—"

Oh dear, thought Eve, with some chagrin, recalling that uncomfortable supper party, the American had not understood Gerald at all, not his humor, nor his casualness, nor his gallantry. And Gerald hadn't even made an attempt to understand the American. She had tried so hard to be a bridge between them. That was what you were for life when you married someone from another country—a bridge. You stretched and stretched yourself to meet both sides and even then half the time no one noticed. No one walked across. That was terrible. The American hadn't noticed she was being a bridge. He had just noticed *her*, in a flattering enough way. She could see he was thinking: I get *you* all right but why in hell did you marry *him?* But that wasn't what she wanted. She wanted them to like each other. She hated being pulled in half, for she understood the American. She warmed to his vivid speech ("Like a bat out of hell"—yes—who but an American would say that?), to his generosity, to his outright honesty, to his sense of reality, of facts, even. He was gallant, too. She could read it in those frank, those beautifully frank, blue eyes. But he was so earnest about it. He wasn't way up in the clouds. He had his feet on the ground. He was earthy, like her. She was willing to bet he would feel the texture of a clod, crumbling under his foot—maybe even better than Gerald.

(Eve glanced guiltily at the brown leather coat in front of her and then quickly away again.) Did Gerald really feel the clod crumbling under his foot? Could he really sink his teeth into the rind of a soft cheese? Not the way *she* did, she was afraid. Not even, she suspected—(There was a cold draft leaking into her mind somewhere.)—not even the way the American did.

What was this thing she called "texture" or "consistency"? Didn't it make up life, the very stuff of living? At least, wasn't it the top crust of living that most people broke through and never noticed at all, never enjoyed? It wasn't all of life, of course; just one layer. To appreciate life, Eve was beginning to realize vaguely, you must take it at all its levels; at its top crust, at its middle everyday layer, and then at some deeper inner core she wasn't quite sure of and couldn't analyze and had only felt once or twice in her life, in great moments. Most people got only the middle layer; children always got the crust; but very few people reached the inner core. Saints, perhaps, and great artists. The rest of people were like her and only felt it once or twice in their lives, when they were in love or sharpened by pain or sorrow, or near death.

Oh—how did you reach that inner core? Eve moved in her hard seat with a kind of anguish. She was greedy for life. She wanted it all—all. She didn't want to miss any of it.

The plane rocked gently. Gerald was wobbling the stick to draw his wife's attention. In the air, Eve responded to that familiar gesture as instinctively, as sharply, as she responded on the ground to his voice speaking her name. It was as personal and as vivid as the touch of his hand on her knee. Startled out of her reverie, she leaned forward to see what it was. He banked the ship over on one wing and pointed out something below them—a French town. But out of that collection of tiled roofs rose a cathedral, erect and fragile as a flower, pushing out of the earth. They often flew over cathedral towns and she always had the same feeling—a shock of delight to see this jewel, held on high by all the low tiled roofs, as if with their hands they held it up to the sky, a gift from earth to heaven. Gerald throttled back the engine and shouted something.

Rheims! It was Rheims, of course. She remembered the war poster of a flaming Rheims she had seen in her father's study as a child—Rheims, bombed and burned by the war. The war again. She looked at the map and saw all around her finger those familiar names: the Marne, Verdun, the Argonne—all those names she had heard as a child dimly resounding above her head at the breakfast table. Old battlefields—a hundred times they had been fought over, wrested back and forth. And Hitler said never again would they fight over that piece of Europe. Hitler said never again would blood be shed—and yet—

No, she would not think of it. She would not look back or ahead. She was with her husband. They were together. She was having a child. She must hang on to life now, taste it, appreciate it to the full. War was behind them, perhaps ahead of them. But *this,* this was *now.* And she must not lose it, not a second of it.

She put away the map and looked out at the sky. The overcast had lifted, yes, but what was that haze ahead of them? Clouds? Fog? There were one or two wisps of clouds, innocent pulled-out bits of cotton wool, floating about here and there at their level. Were these accidental travelers voyaging on their own or did they mean trouble ahead? Probably they were about to hit that "second layer of overcast" the weather man had prophesied. Eve felt slightly chilled looking ahead at the haze. What did it mean?

For she, Eve realized honestly, was not adventurous, not a bit of it. She was an earth-person, attached to earth, attached to life. She wasn't a coward. No. But she knew you were apt to get bumped off if you didn't think about the speed of the foehn winds, about the time, about the weather—all those things. Yes, and she was often afraid, too,—not gallant like Gerald. Not that she ever ran away from the things she was afraid of. You couldn't do that exactly. All you could do when you were afraid was to fill up the hole with something else. At the worst hour it always happened. When the hole got big enough, something rushed in to fill it up. She wasn't responsible for it; she took no credit for it; it just came. It came that time they turned over in Reykjavik harbor. What was it? Not courage; she couldn't tap on courage like that. It was something else. Love, perhaps? No, that was too small a word.

Love and courage both were too small words, human words. And this was something superhuman that came in from the outside—more like ecstasy. Maybe the mystics could describe it?

Why, of course, she thought with some shock, she supposed they would call it God. The non-conformist in her was embarrassed at the word. It was too facile, too easy to use a word like that. It smacked of false religions, the purple edges of religion, not the white nameless blaze itself in the center. But anyway, what did it matter what you called it? It came always at the worst moment.

Only—Eve gave an apprehensive glance at the flocks of clouds, bolder now, coming in packs around them, sizzling against the wing—they weren't at the worst moment yet. Not nearly. No, there was always that long pit of despair to get through before they reached the worst moment—if they were going to get there. But perhaps this time they wouldn't get there. Perhaps it wouldn't be so bad this time. Perhaps it was a broken overcast. Gerald was climbing to get over it. They would still keep ground contact through the holes. Eve sat up straight and felt herself stiffen all over, braced for whatever might come. Just the same, she thought, this was exactly what she didn't want, long hours of sitting stiff. It wasn't good for her.

But if she were afraid—Eve turned on herself honestly—then *why* was she going on this trip? Why, with every excuse to stay home? There was Peter sitting up in bed staring at her. ("Why do you have to go, Mother?") She was having a baby. ("Avoid all stress and strain" said the Mother's Aid book and "The pregnant woman should not travel.") Then why? After all, she was here of her own free will. She certainly wasn't doing it out of wifely devotion. She wasn't that unselfish. No, she was doing it for herself, she had to admit, because of something very strong in herself. A feeling for life, she guessed it was. That was as near as she could come to it. And life was too precious to be wasted.

Life, even solitary life, was too precious to be wasted; but when it was shared with someone else, someone with whom you had understanding—then it became priceless beyond measure. Each instant lived like that was rich and full. If you had only one or two in life, that was something. But to be given eight, nine, ten years—it was incredible. If there were a war, if Gerald were killed, even so—Eve felt with a rush of gratitude —she would be in debt forever to life for what it had given her.

Thank God, she had always realized the value of life; she had never taken it for granted—even before her marriage (this strange existence of deep peace at home and wild trips abroad). But flying had intensified it for her. It was the sense of danger, she supposed, that sharpened your sense of life, the sense of death hovering over you like the shadow of a hawk, ready to pounce upon your joy and take it away from you. This joy, you said, may pass, may cease at any moment. Take it while you can. "The meat is sweetest close to the bone."

People in wartime felt like that, of course, but she

had always had it. And she had only found two other
people who felt it as vividly. There was that English
girl, married to an aviator, who had leaned across a
table and said to a stray remark of Eve's, "It gets more
and more as you go on—like autumn—less and less to
see, but more and more beautiful—the last scarlet berries left on a bush." And Eve had seen it once in the
face of an American woman who had just pulled her
husband through a desperate illness. Perhaps you had
to be married to an aviator or an invalid to have a really
vivid sense of life. Other people had it at moments, in
danger and in emergencies. But we, we—Eve wanted
to touch hands with those other two women—we have
had some veil removed from our eyes. We see death
behind each blade of grass, like a shadow accenting it.
So incredibly beautiful, so sharp, so clear does this
shadow make the blade of grass that one cries out for
joy.

Eve pushed her head up against the rounded hatch
with a wild desire to break through it. The anguish in
her seemed to grow beyond all bounds. It soared like
the flame of a candle trapped in a hurricane lamp.
Achilles, O Achilles, it must be hard to die!

But if life were so precious—(The candle flame
flickered down to its normal size again.)—why not stay
home and look after it? Why not get down on your
knees to Gerald and beg him to stop flying—if life were
so valuable? She certainly wasn't being very logical,
Eve decided. It wasn't her strong point. But she felt
she must think this out. It would help maybe—over the

Alps. Why not beg Gerald to stop flying? Why not stay home and take care of life?

Because, because—Eve stumbled around in her mind for words—that wasn't what she meant by "life" or "death." People "died" all the time in their lives. Parts of them died when they made the wrong kind of decisions—decisions against life. Sometimes they died bit by bit until finally they were just living corpses walking around. If you were perceptive you could see it in their eyes; the fire had gone out. Yes, there were a lot of people walking around who were "dead," and a lot of people killed who were "living." She couldn't explain it any more than that. But you always knew when you made a decision against life. When you denied life you were warned. The cock crowed, always, somewhere inside of you. The door clicked and you were safe inside—safe and dead.

And usually it was fear that made you pull the door shut: emotional fear of becoming involved with people, of loving too much (because it always meant suffering to love deeply, as she loved Gerald and Peter); physical fear of pain and death (if she, for instance, had stayed home from this trip); spiritual fear of the great and the unknown that made you stop in your mind when you came on words like God and Prayer.

You couldn't lay down rules for other people but you knew for yourself when you were turning against life—and when you were going with it.

That was it. And she—Eve felt, coming up from this underground world of thought like a spring bubbling to the surface—she was going with life on this trip.

That was why she was there. Of course. It all seemed quite simple and she felt extremely happy. Like that underground spring suddenly reaching the air, she wanted to sing now in the sunshine. She was going with life.

VI

NO HAWK SO HIGH

AND now, to share this joy—would she have to wait until tonight? It was so long to wait. If only she could just say to Gerald, "I know why I'm here, Gerald, because . . ." But it was impossible for her to make a sound above the engine. He could only just make himself heard by throttling down, pulling the ship up into a stall and then, in that moment's pause, shouting back a few harsh words. And her message would not go on a scratch pad. Putting it down in black and white on a smudged scrap of paper would dissipate it. It would immediately make her discovery small and commonplace, like putting champagne into a lily cup. No, she could not really communicate her joy to him now. The best she could do was to poke him and offer him a sandwich which he would refuse. (He almost never ate when he flew, and he hated cold meat sandwiches.) That was rather silly. But still, that foolish act of passing him the sandwich would be a kind of symbol of participation. And she felt compelled now to share— not only her joy but life, to break the spell that lay over them both and separated them. She wanted to be sure they were both sharing the same life—or the same dream.

She pulled out the lumpy brown-bread sandwich,

wrapped in oiled paper, and gently pushed it against her husband's arm. He did not look at her but, half turning around, glanced down at the sandwich. And then made a face—what a face, as though it smelled to high heaven! Why, even Gubbio, Eve remembered, when he refused a piece of slightly turned meat, was much more polite. Gubbio just turned his aristocratic nose away as though the meat weren't there at all, as though he had been intending all the time to sniff out of that far window. But Gerald—what a face! He enjoyed making it, of course. It showed he was having a good time. He felt happy about life and the trip. And they were no longer separated. They were back in the same world of sights and sounds and smells and sandwiches in waxed paper.

She pulled back the sandwich and began unwrapping it herself. Soggy and cold, it was, and the bacon rather stiff like corrugated cardboard, once wet and dried out again. Maybe Gerald was right. It did seem a sacrilege to chew English bread over France. Maybe tonight they would get a nice crisp crust, or even a rind of runny cheese.

Tonight did not seem so far away. She could let herself anticipate a little. They must be near the border of Switzerland. She looked out hopefully. They were still over a sea of clouds; but it was broken, she noticed with rising spirits. You could look down and suddenly glimpse through a peephole lovely little bits of earth below; a patch of brown field, a green meadow of winter wheat, a church steeple, a stand of trees. She found these broken bits of earth almost more beautiful than

the whole. The field, the trees, the tiny steeple were
set off by their white cloud-frames, like the view from
a small tower-window. They had a gem-like vividness
reminding her of those bits of medieval glass that,
pieced together, make the glowing rose window of a
French cathedral.

But how did Gerald ever piece them together? How
could he make out where they were? In one of the
peephole flashes that passed below her, she noticed a
big river. At least, she thought it was a big river. It
might have been a small one flooded. And what river?
She pulled the map out of the side pocket again. Was
it one of the rivers that ran north into the Meuse and
then on to the North Sea? Or was it one that went south
into the Rhône and down into the Mediterranean? If
it were a Rhône river, that meant they were almost to
the border of Switzerland. Then Gerald was going
straight over the Alps, not around them. They were
certainly climbing. She could tell that from the engine,
even when she couldn't see the ground. She could see,
too, now and then, through the peepholes, patches of
forests on the slopes. Yes, probably he was headed right
toward the Alps. Well, she didn't mind so much; the
weather was certainly better. You could even see
broken patches of sky above, small irregular fragments
of brilliant blue, dazzling counterparts to the earth-
fragments scattered below.

Patches of earth below them, patches of sky above,
and they were in the center. They belonged neither
to earth nor heaven; they were part of this bustling,
shifting, changing world of clouds. They were brothers

to the clouds, hurrying along with them, racing them, following them, bumping shoulders with them, playing tag with them; like a flock of birds all going together, all headed south. She loved this—this was flying: to be part of the sky, not under it or above it or on it, but *of* it, one piece with it, one of the elements that make up "sky." Gerald loved it, too, she knew. They were together in this. She felt they were riding the same horse. She could feel each bound of the canter, each footfall, each hesitation. They rose and fell as one —she and Gerald and the ship.

It was also, she felt, like playing in the surf when the waves were not too big, but big enough to be exciting; when you were not afraid and could dive through them and leap with them and become one of them. There was just that kind of excitement here. There was the slight bump as you dove into a cloud and the sudden blanking out of the world in white nothingness. When this happened, the instrument board in front of Gerald suddenly came to life. All those dull little clocks and meters and hands seemed almost to jump out at her like jack-in-the-boxes. They became real and important and alive then, like human faces registering emotion, surprise, fear and pleasure. You watched them with eagerness; you warmed to their indications as to the smile on the face of a friend. And then—bounce—you were out again in the bright open world of sight and sounds and bits of shifting sky and shifting earth. Then the faces on the instrument board all flattened out; they went back into their niches;

they closed their eyes; they were just inanimate dials and meters, not friends any more.

Yes, this was flying: to be part of the sky, to be racing with the clouds, to be climbing toward those open patches of blue, toward the sun—and the Alps. They must be getting near the Alps, Eve thought. Looking down through the clouds, she could see the green slopes up which they were climbing, covered more and more now with pine forests. The peepholes were no longer peepholes but great gashes torn wide open in the once unbroken blanket of clouds. In fact, there was almost as much clearing as cloud. The patches of blue above them grew wider; the earth was no longer fragmentary but all of a piece again, even though partly hidden.

The weather was definitely clearing. The sun was even coming out. It would warm Eve's shoulder for one delicious moment, blazing unexpectedly through the hatch. It was lighting up the patchwork world below. The earth became alive, burning with contrast and color. The hills were very green and the red-roofed cottages, very red. Their colors were unreal, like freshly painted toys. Lovely toy world of stiff pine trees and green felt slopes and red-roofed dolls' houses. They must have passed France. This was certainly Switzerland. It looked like Switzerland—crisp and clean and bright like an apple.

And there ahead of them, through the shifting cloud layer, she could catch an occasional glimpse of the horizon—mountains, blue in the distance. The Alps, the foothills of the Alps. Yes, they were going straight across. But it was all right in weather like this. The

clouds were thinning out against the mountains. They
ceased to have importance any more. Like the instruments in good weather, they fell back into the inanimate world. Eve no longer felt they were friends or
brothers. They were still climbing through them, not
for the fun of it now; but to get free of them, to get
over them, superior to them, in the unbroken blue
above.

Oh, this was flying, Eve thought: conquering the
weather, conquering the clouds, the sky—yes—and the
Alps, too. For the Alps were ahead. She put on her
dark glasses and peered out. The world was getting too
bright to look at. Not the world, actually, but the sun-
lit tops of the clouds they were riding. There was no
snow yet. Funny, no snow. They must be pretty high
and they were climbing all the time. These were real
hills here, pine-covered and wild. This one they were
headed across now was a mountain. The trees thinned
out halfway up its side. Big hostile outcrops of rock
took their place. And there was snow, patches here and
there, near the top. She felt excited by it, a first glimpse,
a token only, of the challenge ahead. They climbed
with more difficulty over this wall. It was a real barrier
to the world on the other side which they could not
see. But now they were even with it—over it quickly,
after the long climb up. The bare cliffs, the patches of
snow dropped behind. And in front of them, like a gift,
like the fairy tale treasure waiting behind the high
hedge of thorns, lay a blue lake, still and clear, cupped
in green velvet hills.

Gerald pushed a map back at her and his dirty

thumb marked the blackened square of a town—Neuchâtel. Eve looked at her own big map of Europe.
Neuchâtel—they had gained Neuchâtel—as far as that!
She was right; they were in Switzerland, then. She kept
her eyes fixed to the ground now. There was so much
to see: lakes like jewels; neat towns spread out, with
square towers and peaked roofs; rivers, white with
cataracts; railroad lines, threading the valleys. She
could make out where they were by these. The map
came alive. Earth was important now and vivid. She
felt attached to it again. These bright roofs, these steep
towers, these jewel-lakes, these skeins of railroad lines
—all spoke to her and she answered. She was glad they
were there. She belonged to them and they to her. She
was crossing over earth quickly, in a new swift form
of transportation, but it was still hers. She had not lost
it. She was touching it with her fingertips. This was
flying: to go swiftly over the earth you loved, touching
it lightly with your fingertips, holding the railroad
lines in your hand to guide you, like a skein of wool in
a spider-web game—like following Ariadne's thread
through the Minotaur's maze. Where would it lead—
where?

The stiff corner of Gerald's folded map poked her
knee again. He was pointing out another lake. To the
right, quite distant, you could catch a glimpse of it,
misty blue, through the haze. Lake Geneva—a corner
of it. Lake Geneva already! They'd be across Switzerland in no time at this rate. This isn't bad, Eve thought,
with growing confidence. Is this all there is to the Alps?

And then, through the melting mists, a long valley

opened up ahead. Two narrow lakes lay cupped at its end—ice-blue, cloud-blue lakes—shimmering far below them in the sunshine. A wide scattering of houses, too, spread out between the lakes, clinging to their edges like pebbles. Good-sized towns, they were, blackening the valley. She should be able to identify them from her map. Thun, probably, and Interlaken. And beyond —she peered through the shifting mists— Heavens, she thought, could *those* be the Alps? For beyond, tower-ing into the clear sunshine and dazzling blue, far above them, a wall of white peaks shot up dizzyingly high. The horizon had suddenly leapt to the clouds. *Are* they clouds? Eve wondered, incredulous for a moment. They can't be mountains, way up there in that other realm. For the foothills and lower slopes, dark with shadows and pine trees, seemed to bear no relation to that ethereal line of white peaks floating above them.

Can those be—yes—those must be—the Alps. Blue-white iridescent peaks. Surely they were not made of the same substance as the rest of earth. They must be born of sky. Sun, blue atmosphere, and clouds had nur-tured them, not earth at all.

So those were the Alps. Eve took a deep breath and pinned her eyes on them, forgetting the world below, which a moment before had meant so much to her. She could only look at the Alps. This was the barrier they must cross; these were the giants they must assail; this was the realm—this pure unearthly realm—they must reach.

But how—how could they? Eve felt acutely humble. "What is man, that thou art mindful of him?—what is man—" How can we assail them, she thought, taking their measure with her eye—just us, in this frail little earth-plane, this flimsy bit of plywood and steel, tossed in the wind? How can we ever climb up to them, surpass them even? How arrogant of us to think that we, gnat-like, can go against these gods.

And yet she knew they must. This was the challenge. This was all that mattered now. The lakes, the towns, the railroad lines she had been holding in her hand— all dropped below in insignificance. They could no longer help her. They ceased to have importance any more, like the clouds. They must be left behind. She must let go of earth. Only the Alps mattered.

Fixing their eyes on the peaks they climbed slowly. Drawn to that distant mark, nothing in between counted. In seven-league-boots they were striding across the valley, scarcely noticing what lay at their feet. The lower pine-treed slopes, the snowy valleys, the icy gorges, one by one fell behind them. Slowly they pulled themselves up into the realm of the giants. It was cold, but the sun was a warm and brilliant cloak on their shoulders, a reward for their efforts, a token of their entrance into the upper spheres. The clouds, pale wisps, were far below them. And farther below still, sunk in some dim underworld, shimmered a lake like a lost coin.

Had they climbed so high, then? Eve felt their height like solid gain beneath them. But one must not measure by the distance down, she knew; but by the distance up. How far up had they climbed? How much had they gained on the giants? They were up to their shoulders, she thought. They were nearing those snowy sides. They could see, now, what lay below the snow, the infernal black outcrops of rock, the long, bony skeletons of the mountains. But they must climb beyond the shoulders, up to the very brows. They must be equal to the giants. Oh, if only they could be a little more than equal. If only they could look down on the giants—what that would be—to soar above them, to cease to be afraid of them, to let the giants, too, drop below as unimportant.

But no, Gerald seemed to think they were high enough. They were setting out across the mountains now, going right up to those sheer peaks. "Flying in the face of the Lord," it was. How did they dare? They were equal to the giants, then; all but the very highest, a pointed wicked peak, white like an iceberg, butting its head alone into the blue. They were up to the brows of the giants, those smooth imperturbable brows. They were rounding those craggy sides. They were coasting over dazzling sheets of something whiter than snow; sheer surfaces of ice, glacier, and snow that bore no relation to ice, glacier, and snow because they were so pure, untouched, and incomparable to anything in man's world. Around the heads of the giants the plane wheeled, alone like a hawk rounding a solitary peak. But no hawk would venture so high.

Eve tingled with excitement. Ah, this, this was flying —to leave the clouds below; to let go of earth, to touch it no longer, not even with your fingertips; no Ariadne thread to guide you, no silken skein to join you to earth. To abandon earth utterly and climb into the upper reaches of sky; to meet the mountains eye to eye; to set off across them; to salute them as you passed. Not arrogantly—no, she had no arrogance left in her—but in awe. "What is man, that thou art mindful of him? . . . Thou hast made him a little lower than the angels." "A little lower," that was all. But still, lower. She looked on the mountains with reverence. She blinked as she stared into the white light of their faces. There were no words to say before them. How beautiful, she started to say, blinded by a fall of white. How terrible, she finished in the same breath. Oh, how terrible and how beautiful! And terror and beauty were one.

Terror, because she could never forget where they were, balanced up there on those dizzy heights. On what? On the blast of an engine, those little putt-putts syncopating clearly in the thin air. That was what held them up there, their cheeks against the icy beards of the giants. Balanced on the blast of an engine, they were. What a feat of acrobatics and how perilous. Like the angels balanced on the point of a needle, they were balanced on the blow of an engine. If that should fail, where would they be? They would fall; they would crash, on those cold unearthly heights; a speck of black on the white beard, that would be all.

Yes, only by the grace of God were they there, balanced on a needle's point, balanced on the blast of an engine, on the flutter of a wing. But only from such a vantage point could one feel the beauty—the terrible beauty—of the mountains. It was her terror before the mountains that made them real and not just picture postcards in an album of Swiss scenery. No, they were real; they were life. And she could sense their reality because she was afraid, because she knew death was so close. The nearness to death made life more alive, and beauty more beautiful. "The meat is sweetest close to the bone."

On and on, through these white passes, skidding around their precipice drops, coasting over their snow fields, wheeling, turning, gliding. They were in and out among the peaks now, playing around them, it seemed to Eve, drawn to them, like a moth to a flame. They kept just far enough off to be safe, always the same distance, as though some inexorable law held them there, like the bonds that held the planets wheeling about the sun. She had a sense, too, that, like the planets, they were following a definite rhythm or pattern in their flight. They seemed to be doing figure eights, dancing, she felt, smoothly and beautifully over polished floors.

It was flying no longer. What was it? Skating, perhaps. That was it. They were skating on this perilously thin ice, this beautiful crystal surface. Swiftly, swiftly they must go; lightly, lightly they must turn, not stopping, not hesitating for an instant. Wheeling, turning, waltzing on that polished mirror, which could crack at any moment, breaking the dance, the pattern. Oh, then they would be dancers no longer, no longer light-footed and swift. They would fall into those black abysses below. The wings on their feet would become iron weights to drag them down, down.

But no—oh no—the ice would not crack; they would

not fall; they would not stop, not for an instant. They knew their safety lay in their speed, in their lightness, in the perfect taut harmony of sway and bend and turn. Their skates kissed the ice softly as they wheeled and spun, doing their figure eights in time. Their breath came and went sharply in unison as they kept up this seemingly effortless effort. With the chill air on their faces and their hands locked in partnership, they would go on and on forever, like this, Eve felt, across those fields of crystal no man had cut before. They would strike out over the black ice noiselessly, rhythmically, leaving behind them only the eddies of air from their heels; only the faint etched marks of their skates, curling behind them in the distance—like signatures.

Oh, did he know—Gerald—? thought Eve, sitting taut in her seat. Did he feel it too? She wanted again to touch him, to find out, to share. Did he realize they were skating hand in hand over heavenly ice? Did he feel the rhythm to which they danced? Did he see the smooth untouched surfaces ahead of them over which no skater had set foot before, no man had gone?

Though, of course, Eve remembered, abruptly coming back to earth, that was foolish. Of course, men had crossed the Alps before, thousands of times, through tunnels and by air and how many times painfully over the passes by foot. Why, Hannibal crossed the Alps, Hannibal and his elephants. What—right here? Surely not. These sheer peaks, these blinding snow fields, these blue-shadowed glacial gullies? Those poor elephants from Africa. How long it must have taken. How slow and painful and plodding and frost-bitten—while she and Gerald could fly, could dance, could skate across the Alps.

Oh, she must touch him. She must share this joy of being equal with the giants, of being "a little lower than the angels," of dancing, of skating hand in hand over the Alps. But it would not go on a pad. Oh no. Then, impulsively she took the little block of paper out of her pocket and wrote down with tingling fingers, clumsy in their sheath of mittens and gauntlets: "Hannibal took his elephants over the Alps." She pushed it forward, a little tremulously, and sat bolt upright watching the side of her husband's face, the helmet bent over the pad, the pause while he looked, and then the sudden gesture of his head thrown back in laughter. He was laughing at her, with her.

A current of delight hummed through Eve. Yes, he understood; they had touched—where Hannibal took his elephants—over the Alps.

VII

THE ANTEROOM

THEY were over the Alps. At least, they must be over the worst of them. They were still dancing around the glassy peaks and skidding down the snow fields but there were no new hurdles ahead. They could leap any that appeared, Eve felt confident; they were so high. They had passed over France, over Switzerland, over the clouds, over the valleys, now even over the giants. With such height one was free, all-powerful, all-seeing. One felt oneself a god. No wonder Satan tempted Christ from a mountaintop with the world spread out at his feet, like this. For she began to see vistas ahead now. Behind the peaks were more peaks with a few stray clouds clinging to the tops. Beyond the white valleys were more valleys opening up, dappled here and there with cloud shadows. Eve noted casually this reappearance of clouds. The giants had shaken them off their shoulders, pushed up beyond them except for an occasional white plume wreathing an icy peak like a crown. But in the valleys ahead there were scattered clouds breaking up the surface of the snow with their shadows. Earth shadows and sky shadows mingled confusedly on the bright slopes. They did not really concern Eve. Nothing concerned her at the moment, with the sun on her shoulders. In fact, she took the clouds as a good omen, another sign that they were reaching the other side of the Alps. Probably there would be broken clouds butting up against the Italian side of the Alps just as there had been on the French side. It didn't matter as long as they were broken, as long as there was no fog. She rather enjoyed scattered clouds. It was the kind of sky she liked best, not too monotonously clear—a sky with texture to it. Besides, with such height—they were far above the valleys and the clouds—they were invulnerable. They were, after all, over the Alps.

Eve pressed her head against the window and peered down at the ground below. She was dimly aware of something different about this valley they were crossing now. A new element had entered, like a new instrument inconspicuously taking its place in the orchestra. What was it? She could not make out at first and then, all at once, she knew: pine trees. Their stiff prickly outlines were beginning to venture a short way up the steep slopes. How black they looked etched against fields of white. The first pine trees. They must be over the crest then. She was right. They were leaving the realm of the giants. Now they would start to go down, down into Italy.

Like a sailor, after days at sea, watching the first signs of land—new birds, seaweed on the water, fishing boats—she noted eagerly those first signs of a return to earth. In the next valley there were roofs, snow-covered. She could hardly see the houses themselves but the sharp black corners of eaves and the unnatural angles of the shadows, slanting like dominoes off in-

visible walls, betrayed the tidy hand of man. Even the
white fields began to look tidy. The snow had erased all
boundary lines. She could see no fences; but the tops
of the posts remained, sticking up through the drifts
in dotted rows like French-knot embroidery, marking
off one neighbor's pocket-handkerchief of snow from
another's. Here was a coal-black river slicing its way
through snowy banks. And here abruptly they came on
a railroad, two black lines drawn over a white paper
landscape. They followed it, chased through a cut in
the valley after it. She held it in her hand until it disappeared into a black mouse hole on the side of one
of the mountains. Now they were in a long dark valley,
not green but snowless and many-roofed. The ground,
after the white valleys behind them, looked dirty with
roofs, and the dingy color spread part way up the
mountain sides, until finally its spotted gray blended
into the white expanses of the upper heights. This was
a real town. There was a railroad junction and a river
with bridges crossing it. They were back in man's
world again. They were on their way down, down the
Alps into Italy.

Gerald turned the plane into the valley, following
the river and the railroad line. But the roofs, so
crowded at the junction, straggled along halfheartedly
here and soon petered out altogether. The dirt receded.
The snow encroached again on the sides of the gulley.
And the railroad line disappeared entirely. Where had
it gone? Down another mouse hole? Trains were lucky,
Eve thought. They could go anywhere. "The little cat
feet" of the fog never caught them. She started look-

ing around for the mouse hole when suddenly the valley slid out from under her eye. Oh, they were banking, up on one wing. Why? She wondered, mildly
curious. It must have been the wrong valley, just a
spur valley, not the main one. Oh well (From the luxury of her security—for surely they were over the Alps,
over the worst now, on the way down into Italy—she
forgave Gerald easily this little mistake.), he must be
having trouble finding the tortuous path they were
supposed to take through the fortified zones.

They were now following the river in the opposite
direction. The valley broadened; the river grew wider.
Ah, yes, Eve thought with confidence, this must be the
right way. She found a tributary stream running into
the main river. They were going downstream, then.
That was right; the river must go to the sea, the Mediterranean. They were going down, down into Italy.

There were clouds ahead though, quite a number
in the valley, floating about at their height, blocking
off their view. Eve's brow puckered with annoyance.
What clouds were these? Where did they come from?
Were they the same "scattered clouds" she had looked
down on from their great height a few minutes ago?
Were they on the same level now? Had they lost so
much altitude? The clouds were still "scattered," of
course; you could see between them. But they were
rather annoying just the same—got in your way. She
didn't like having to duck mountains and clouds at
the same moment. It was confusing. You might mistake
one for the other. Still, the valley was getting wider,
flattening out. Soon—

The brown leather coat stirred in the front cockpit. Gerald was looking at his maps, checking the fortified zones, looking out at the valley. He shook his head. Oops—they were up on one wing again. The valley slid off at an angle. He was turning around. Now really, Gerald, what's this all about? Eve no longer felt carelessly indulgent.

Gerald turned around as if in self-defense. "Following wrong valley," he shouted back, somewhat superfluously, it seemed to her. Why waste his breath on that obvious statement? She could see for herself they were in the wrong valley. Where was the right one? That was the question, and how much time had they lost? There were peaks and clouds all about them now. They were up to their necks in the darned things. "This is a terrible place to get lost in!" she shouted back angrily to the empty air. Of course he could not hear her, but it made her feel better. She set her mouth in a hard little grimace. I'll be needing that Saint Bernard yet, she thought.

They started to follow another valley. But halfway down they met the clouds again. Clouds? Eve straightened to awareness as she peered out at the barrier ahead of them. The neck of the valley was completely covered, filled up with white billows, choked by them— a mass of white rounded backs, all the same, immobile, stubborn, clogging off the road in front of them like a flock of stupid sheep. Eve stiffened as she took careful stock of the situation. These were no mere clouds. They looked more like—a frown settled on her face— fog. There was nothing broken about them, nothing accidental. They were no stray travelers out on their own, no companions in the air, playing with flyers and mountain peaks alike. No, this was something else. This small bowlful of fluff in the gully, this innocent pile of cotton wool in the corner—it was a danger sign. It was the vanguard, perhaps, of a new enemy. It might be an overflow, spilling into the valley from some vast sea outside; like a small tongue of glacier, forced down into a crevasse from the mammoth ice-cap hidden behind. What that ice-cap was like, that mass beyond her vision, she could only guess from her safe vantage point on the edge. But she knew there was no passage through. This was a dead end. One could only turn back or climb above. It was clear, of course, behind them. She felt the bright air they had just cut across like a bag of gold in reserve. And it was clear above.

She glanced up through the dome of glass over her head. Oh, there was that layer of scattered clouds, still playing about the peaks, above them now. Had they sunk so low? They were below both peaks and clouds. All their precious altitude was lost. What had Gerald done with it? Wasted it all in those fruitless valleys? What was he thinking of, she fretted with rising irritation, to throw it about like that? Ah—they were beginning to climb again. Eve took a deep breath. Well, it was time they did, she went on scolding Gerald mentally. This was not the place to play about in unless you had lots of altitude, unless you had plenty of time, slowly gliding down—if anything went wrong—to pick your spot to land. And, even then, where would they land? There wasn't a level spot to be found. The houses themselves were perched on the sides of hills. Those feather-etched pine trees would be prickly to sit on. Those innocent French-dot embroidery fence posts would trip up a plane that tried to roll across them. No, they would have to climb to safety. Thank goodness, it was clear above.

Up, up into the cold heights. Like a diver under water, they swam up to the free air where they could once more see and breathe. Up through the layer of scattered clouds. No longer so scattered, it seemed to Eve, as they pushed up through the fizzy cotton-wool mists. This was an ocean of clouds they were climbing past, a layer of entangling seaweed the diver must butt his head through before he could be free. Maybe it wasn't even a clear-cut layer. These scattered clouds, weren't they simply the upper level of the fog bank in the valley? The outlying members of a larger cohesive mass? The flying fish that had somehow got loose from their mother sea but were actually one with it, blended into it here and there, indistinguishable, really, from it? It was all one bank of fog they would have to get above.

Oh, here they were out. They were even with it now, their heads free of the seaweed. They could breathe again and see. But what could they see? Eve looked out anxiously across waves of placid, motionless white billows, pierced through occasionally with still whiter peaks, ominous reminders of the wicked shoals hidden beneath that deceptively calm surface. She was right, then; it was just one mass. She couldn't find any holes. And they were going over it? Single-engine, no radio, no parachutes—and they were going over the stuff? Now Gerald— Eve felt the first pricks of panic rising in her. But she fought them back quickly. Well, it would be broken further on, probably, like the other side, she reasoned with herself. And then, of course, they would be going down all the time now, down into Italy. The hot Italian sun would burn the fog away.

They weren't going down yet. They were still climbing to gain altitude. She didn't grudge that. The higher they were, the better. They were still rounding peaks. She didn't want to run any chance of ramming into one by accident, running head on against "a stuffed cloud." No, thank you. With each foot of altitude she breathed more easily. It was good to get high, to jump over the barrier, the way they jumped over the Channel with always enough height to be able to glide down to shore if the motor cut. She supposed they'd pick up the pass again on the other side. The other side of what? Of the clouds? Suppose there were no "other side"? Eve looked back hastily. Well, anyway, there were still open valleys behind. They could always glide back to them. Even though there were no level fields, you could at least see to pick out your spot for a crash landing. Gerald always said he could land anywhere "without serious trouble"—as long as he could see. As long as he could see, Eve repeated nervously. She would just hang on to those valleys for good measure, not let them go from her hand until there was something to touch on the other side.

It was very cold. But it shouldn't be long now. Soon they should be going down into Italy and warmth.

Funny, Eve thought, she hadn't felt cold over the Alps.
At least, she couldn't remember feeling cold. She could
only remember her ecstasy and warmth skating over
those dizzy heights. Perhaps there was some connection
between ecstasy and warmth. Joy warmed you; and
fear made you feel cold. Sometimes hunger did too.
Maybe, she thought hopefully, she wasn't really cold,
just hungry. She would try to get out that chocolate.
After all, what was the use of being outfitted like a
Saint Bernard if you didn't take advantage of it.

She pulled off her outer leather gauntlets. She could
never manipulate buttons in those fur-lined paws: her
fingers were clumsy enough in the silk and wool gloves
underneath. She felt for the buttons of her hip pocket.
She couldn't move them. But surely—? No, it was like
a dream. She fumbled and fumbled, not knowing what
was the matter. But I must, I must, she panted angrily.
How her fingers burned. She seemed to have no control
over them any more. Now they were just numb. They
had ceased to feel at all, buttons or pain or anything.
Too cold. Well, it was useless then. She stuck her hands
quickly inside her suit. Feeling came back, tingling
pain. That was better than nothing. She wiggled her
arms up and down. Gradually the pain ebbed away.
A drop from her nose fell on her flying suit and turned
to ice. Those poor elephants, Eve thought inconsequently, gazing on that tiny pellet of ice—what it must
have been like for them. Did they have footballs of ice
dropping off their noses? The thought made her smile.
It was too bad she couldn't tell Gerald. He would draw
her a picture of the elephants with footballs on the

ends of their noses. But it was too cold to write a note. It was too cold to unbutton buttons. She'd have to do without the chocolate. Have to wait for that Saint Bernard. Anyway for Italy. For they must be going down soon, down into Italy, nice warm Italy.

Gradually the peaks floated away behind them. No jagged icebergs pierced the even sea of clouds ahead— wave after wave of gray motionless clouds—for there was no sun, now, to light their crests. A third layer of overcast shut out the sky above. Eve had hardly noticed its approach, so intent had she been on the billows below. But far above them in the firmament, thin washes of cirrus cloud, laid one on top of the other, had gradually veiled the blue. So silken smooth were these level sheets of gray—not rolling and crested like the tops of the cumulus waves below—that one forgot they were clouds. So thin, so light, so high, one scarcely felt their weight on the shoulders. Only they separated one from the sun. Eve minded this vaguely. She liked to feel the warmth on her shoulders. She looked wistfully up at the great gray tent above her from time to time, hoping to find a bright place breaking through. It was slit occasionally by long streaks of blue, very pale, not like the confident blue Swiss sky. There were no glimpses of earth below. She had even lost her open valleys. She had let go of her railroad lines. Looking back, she could only see a darker patch in the sea of clouds to show where they once had been. But the plane could never glide back so far.

What would Gerald do now if the engine cut? Pancake through—blind—on a mountain? No alternative—

no parachutes. Eve fought back her rising panic and irritation. Thought we weren't going to do this kind of flying. This is exactly the sort of thing I shouldn't do. This is just what I didn't want. Even if we get out of it safely, it's dreadful for me. (She felt cold and a little dizzy and very tense.) "The pregnant woman should avoid all stress and strain." Phrases from the Mother's Aid book rang in her ears. "The father should show consideration." Consideration—Heavens! To fly at all was crazy, just plain crazy, and to climb these chute-the-chutes! What would the doctors say? "The giant racer at Wembley is not the place for the pregnant woman." The prim words once heard in a doctor's office danced before her now with a kind of drunken hilarity. How about the Alps, Doctor? How about roller-coasting the Alps? She laughed and felt rather better.

After all, she reasoned, they would probably hit a hole before long and go down, into Italy and warmth. Shadows ridged this blanket of clouds, as though there were cracks in it, holes through which one might see the solid dark of earth below. Eve picked out the darkest shadows ahead and waited eagerly for them to open up beneath her. But when they passed below, they were always just shadows, troughs in the waves of this frozen, colorless sea. Probably, she argued, this cloud bank is just over the mountains, accumulates on them, breaks up against their wall. Wonder how long the mountains take to flatten out after the Alps—flatten out into Italy? Was Italy flat, though? Doubts assailed her. She had never been to Italy and had only the vaguest idea of the country from pictures and books. "The hill towns of Italy—" No, probably not flat, then. But it must be flat around Rome—the Pontine marshes, where the old Romans caught malaria. They were going down all the time, anyway, she reassured herself. It was getting warmer. She could even take her hands out of the gauntlets without their getting numb.

But she didn't feel much like eating chocolate. There was no change in the frozen sea, stretching endless ahead. Always those shadowed troughs that looked like holes and were just troughs when you came to them. Always that dull, overcast sky, streaked now and then with lighter patches, not very blue, pale and bloodless. It threw a cold and watery light over the world—strange light which belonged neither to night nor day, but reminded one of the long, gray, northern twilights. Those stiff cloud rollers ahead of them might be the ghostly shapes of the ice-pack stretching on and on through an unexplored polar ocean. Strange landscape that belonged neither to earth nor sky. They might be on the trackless wastes of the moon, she felt, or perhaps strayed into the ken of another planet, so cut off were they, so alone, so isolated from the world of man in this cold twilit zone.

Twilit? Surely it wasn't as late as that? Eve felt another twinge of uneasiness. What time was it? Where was the sun? She had forgotten about time, the way one forgets a casual and intermittent pain which has disappeared, one hopes, for good. Now it had started throbbing again. It wasn't a bad pain, just a little one in that same old place, but she was irritated to have it catch at her again. She pushed back the cuff of her clumsy mittens and glanced at her wrist-watch. Three-thirty, she noted with some concern. The day was getting on. Suddenly they had eaten over half the pie. When? How? Where had it gone? Of course, they had wasted time. She thought back with bitterness and complete lack of logic at the time Gerald had wasted. That hour at the airport, waiting for the customs man. He couldn't help that, of course, she realized, absolving him grudgingly. But the five minutes on the road looking at the modern house, and the minute spent looking at the new Falcon; that half-hour lost in the valley—those two valleys. It must have been three-quarters of an hour—maybe a whole hour. That was inexcusable—so careless of Gerald. Why was he so imprecise?

Eve looked with rising anger at his stupid, unmoving, complacent, brown leather back. That American, now, would never make a mistake like that. He wouldn't waste a moment. He would never get into this kind of a mess. And if he did, he'd know how to get out. He'd look around and see what he could do. He'd be practical. That's the way Americans were. They—

She sat up straight, roused by her anger to action, took off her dark glasses—maybe that was the trouble—and peered out. This sea must end somewhere. She watched the horizon for some sign of solid earth, a darker patch that would mean a hole, or even a dark peak. She studied the seamless tent above for some change in it—that great gray overcast shutting out the whole sky. No, not quite all of it. There was a little streak of blue far ahead of them, just a crack, as though someone had been careless and forgot to fasten the shutter down tight. That narrow crack left open was clear and light, like a window. Perhaps when we get there, Eve thought hopefully, it will be clear below too. She could remember other times (How easy to sink into the soft bed of memory!) when they had come out of bad weather as abruptly as that. All the clouds had stopped, petered out, like scattered sheep on a hillside. And the blue sky and green earth stretched ahead of them—"unlimited." And Gerald had looked back then and laughed. Oh, perhaps they would come out like that onto Italy. (She let herself sink gently into this delicious feather bed of dreams.) It would be beautiful and sunny, warm and bright, like dropping into another world, a kind of promised land, a new and golden morning. Perhaps—

But how far away it was—that light streak. They did not seem to get any nearer to it and they had been flying toward it for hours. It never got any closer; it never grew any bigger; it never changed. It just stayed there, distant, unattainable, leading them on like a will-o'-the-wisp. She'd better not pin all her hopes on it, Eve thought skeptically; she'd better find something closer. She strained her eyes, with and without her glasses, trying to cut through the haze to find something solid.

All at once she seemed to make out, through the haze, the cold blue of a lake, one of those translucent mountain lakes that suddenly deepen out of the mist. She

could see the shores of it, the hills around it, dimly
but unmistakably. She wanted to cry for joy; it was
such a relief. It had been so long, an hour or more
drifting on the insecurity of this empty markless sea
of cloud. A lake! She pawed at her map clumsily.
Those famous Italian lakes, of course. Lake Maggiore,
Lake Como, perhaps. Near Milan they would be, then.
Oh, she thought, her spirits bouncing back sanguinely,
if that is a lake, I will eat a piece of chocolate. She
looked again. No, it was not a lake. It was sky, a streak
of sky, pale blue. No, not a lake—but surely those were
hills? They were dark; they didn't move. She kept her
eyes on them, trying to detect movement, trying to
watch a certain bump and pin it down. But she did not
know. Was it weariness in her eyes? The outline
seemed to change imperceptibly as she watched. She
gave it up. She looked for another one. This next one
was a real hill, a line of hills, the Apennines, perhaps.
And Gerald probably knew where he was; he was following them down; he could see better in front—

Finally she stopped looking at the hills. She couldn't
bear it. They were going to change, too. She knew it
without looking. That was not a real lake and these
were not real hills. They looked real but they weren't.
They were like those steaming dishes offered one in
dreams that melt at a touch; or like those poisoned
apples in fairy tales that witches use to tempt prin-
cesses—so glowing, so firm, so rosy that one is tempted
in one's terrible need to stretch out one's hand, even
though one knows they contain only the seeds of death.

No, she would not look at them any more. She did

not want to be tempted. She was shaken by the lake
episode. She was afraid. She faced it now: she was
afraid. She recognized all the signs by which fear be-
trays itself before one is willing to look it in the face—
the cold, the irritation, the self-pity, the condemnation
of others, the rationalization, the dreams, the memo-
ries, the mirages—it was all just fear. This was again
one of those tight spots in flying—of anxiety, of tension,
of hanging on. She did not blame Gerald any more.
After all, he couldn't help it—those fortified zones. And
anyway it was just flying. There were always times like
this, situations like this. They couldn't promise to
keep you out of them. He said he wouldn't get into
anything bad, but he couldn't help it. It was just flying; she should have known better. It was her fault, not
his; it was her choice.

After all, as somebody once said, for women there
were two kinds of men in the world—"Those who
are born to understand us and those who are born to
protect us." She had chosen. She had understanding.
You couldn't go back on your choice when you were
over the Alps and wish for a strong he-man from the
West who would keep "the little woman" safe at home
when she was expecting "an addition to the family."
She couldn't go back on understanding, on Hannibal's
elephants with the footballs of ice at the ends of their
noses.

No, she couldn't blame Gerald. She only blamed
herself. She should have known better. It was her fault
for being so stupid. But though the nauseating self-
pity had left her and though the equally nauseating

condemnation of her husband had been replaced by condemnation of herself, this did not give her much satisfaction. Her present bitterness at herself did not help her any more than her former bitterness at Gerald. The hair-shirt of "I have no one to blame but myself" was cold comfort.

And she was still afraid, trembling with fear or cold—she did not know which. Perhaps Gerald would say it wasn't anything to be frightened about. Lots of times he had laughed at her fears, afterwards. "You thought that was a tight spot?" He would laugh at her as a parent who knows better laughs at the fears of a child. "Oh no," he would smile confidently, "I knew where we were all the time." She had a longing now to be a child, to put all her fears on an older and stronger person's shoulder. Oh, she had a longing for a shoulder, to put her head on her husband's shoulder. Maybe she could just tap his shoulder and ask for a word of comfort. It might be right there, for the asking. She could put her hand out and touch it. The temptation was very great, like the temptation when one was afraid of the dark as a child, after hours of lying stiff in one's lonely bed, to open the door and climb into the warm safe bed of your mother and drop off into immediate, deep, secure sleep. It was there for the asking; she had only to put out her hand. She could so easily—and yet—

And yet, if he were really in a tight spot, she considered, regretfully saying good-bye to her vision, it wouldn't help any to have her sniveling in the back seat for comfort. If he saw how afraid she was, if he felt it, even—the fear, the lack of faith—how discouraging for him, how unforgivable. No, she finished firmly, obviously it was unthinkable. The dream of comfort slid behind her, like the lakes, like the poisoned apples. No, but she could write a note, a bravado note, showing him she knew they were "in it," yet laughing a little. She pulled off the clumsy gauntlets energetically and wrote in a bold black hand, "Where do you think we are—over the Mediterranean? Have we gas enough to go on to Egypt? Good weather there!" She drew a round, smiling, pumpkin face after the message to show him it was supposed to be funny.

He did not turn around but smiled and shook his head slowly. Then, after a moment's hesitation, he shouted back at her, "We're not over the Mediterranean." It was not an answer with much heart in it. So he did not know where they were, and he was worried. They were "in it." Eve read all that at a glance. He had given her no comfort, not a crumb; but she felt, surprisingly enough, considerably better, much less afraid, stronger. The straight pole inside herself stiffened again. She sat up, challenged.

Well, we're in it, she thought flatly. She could even take a kind of zest in saying so. See if I can find some land. Perhaps I can see something he doesn't. (She was the grown-up now and he, the child. It was better to be grown-up, even if it meant carrying more.) Again that long searching of the horizon; again the painstaking examination of the "mountains" that kept swimming into view. But she must test them thoroughly, she thought, disciplining her hopes, before giving them to him. Oh, how she would like to present him with a mountain—a real mountain! There was a rush of warmth about her heart as she thought about it. What a gift it would be—a mountain on her palm. But it must be a real one, real and earthy with rocks and pine trees; no steaming dream dishes that melted at touch; no poisoned apples to stick in the throat.

Oh no, she knew what false hopes cost, what they took from you, how they drained from your hoard of confidence like a hidden rat hole in a sack of grain. You didn't know it was there until you picked up the sack and found it disastrously light. She would protect him; she would save him from premature hopes. He must not go through what she had gone through. He needed all his strength—and there was nothing so weakening as a premature hope. She had not forgotten how much strength you lost as a child, swimming in to-ward shore over your depth, when you tried to put your foot down before the bottom was there.

A solid mountain, oh God, to rest upon. She felt like Noah's raven. What wouldn't she give for a mountain. Though Heaven knew what they would do with a mountain if they *did* find one. They couldn't light on it like a raven; they couldn't beach on it like the Ark. At least, it would be something real to feast their eyes upon. They might even be able to slide down it, keeping ground contact all the time, toboggan down to a ceiling and safety. But how did you set about catching a mountain? With what did you snare one? And how to pin it down and ascertain its validity? She needed some better instruments, like the spectroscopes they had in observatories to break up the light from the stars and determine their substance. She had only her tired eyes, the side of a wing and the perpendicular bracing of the hatch, to use as a measure. She tried to frame the mountains into this right angle, to trap them in this artificial sextant and then, furrowing her brows and holding her breath, she would try to detect the slightest deviation, the most delicate wavering or blurring of the outline. But the plane vibrated and turned slightly from time to time. Her mountains would slide out of their frames, and she could never get them back exactly into the same place, or, when she did, remember their peculiar bumps, especially as they were so far away and hazy.

At last she felt she had some genuine mountains. She had put them through a series of rigid tests. They passed the regulations and did not seem to change. She felt, too, that she had turned down so many false mountains, had disciplined herself for so long that she had merited a little indulgence in hope. She scribbled hastily on her pad, "That *must* be land there—it stays the same," and pushed it forward eagerly. Gerald looked at the note, turned his head sharply in the direction she pointed, but did not alter his course. Why didn't he say something? she thought impatiently, longing for some response. She pointed to another ridge on the other side. He looked again but said nothing. They went on straight ahead. Eve felt fuzzy in the head now. Her judgment was going. She was fooling herself. What was even worse—it knocked at her inside somewhere, like the stumble of a child at her hand—she was fooling Gerald. She had handed him a poisoned apple. But he had not taken it. He knew better than she, she reflected humbly. He knew what she now finally realized, the mountains were not real—none of them—no, nor the lakes. Dream mountains, dream lakes, dream harbors, ports they would never reach and could not land at. Lily fields in the sky. Another world. Cerulean.

There was only that patch of light left, still that streak of clear sky gleaming far ahead on the horizon. A tiny slit in the overcast, translucent blue, pale and gold-tinged, beckoning them on. Clear, like one of those clear skies from which all the sediment has slowly sifted down, leaving a crystal fluid through which one can see the tiniest detail for miles. Eve stared hypnotized at that slit of sky as though half expecting the details to open up before her eyes. She knew what form they would take. She could picture one of those idyllic landscapes that stretch away behind the Italian Madonnas. Oh, if they could only get there, would they too not see the little silver stream threading its appointed way down the step-like rocks; the medieval spires in the distance, pricking God's sky with their prayers; the brown hill town on its knees; and that eternally winding road, smooth as a child's ribbon, up which the pilgrims, tiny figures leaning on their crooked staffs, trudged their way in reverence?

"They climbed the steep ascent of heaven"—the old hymn rang in her ears—"through peril, toil, and pain." —Ah, yes—but if one were certain, certain— "O God, to us may grace be given . . ." Was that world waiting for them? Was it there? Could she believe in it? It was all that was left, their only way out, a last hope, that window to the world—if it were true, if it were there, if they could believe in it. But it took such faith, to pin all one's hopes onto that one sliver of light, on that slender bar of gold. Her hopes were too heavy; they would tip the scales. She had not enough faith. It took an almost Biblical faith to fly, to let oneself be led along blindfold by a narrow thread in the hand, to set one's foot, confident, across the waters. She longed for the faith of a Joshua—storming at the walls of Jericho with only a trumpet—or Gideon with his handful of men clashing their buckets and lanterns—or even the faith of a medieval pilgrim trudging up a hill. ("They climbed the steep ascent of heaven . . .") She longed now, not only to see the little landscape behind the Madonna, but to enter it, to be trudging ("Through peril, toil, and pain . . .") up the rippling ribbon road with the pilgrims, brown-cloaked and staff in hand, certain of her destination. ("O God, to us may grace be given—to follow in their train . . .")

But she was not a pilgrim; she could not "follow in their train"; she was not inside the landscape. She was outside, eternally looking at it, journeying toward it, watching it with appraising eyes. That golden streak—it had the gentleness and pallor of evening about it. Would it wait for them? Would they have time to reach it? Oh, time, time—that old pain stabbed at her again. Surely they had time; she fought desperately for it. Why, it could only be about four. She turned back her cuff apprehensively. Yes, only just after four. Why, four o'clock. At home now (With a twinge of anguish to think how separated she was from that life.), she would be setting out with Peter for a walk. Over the stile and across the muddy meadow with a clear hour of English twilight ahead—maybe even more—why, in England— She pulled herself back from that delicious dream, so distant now and unattainable. Unattainable as another world, as those lily fields in the sky, or the golden landscape beyond the Madonna.

In England, yes, *in England*—but this was Italy. Was the time the same here? My God, she realized with a shock, the blood rushing to her head at the discovery, they were going east all the time! They had lost almost an hour. The day was done, practically over. The whole of it fell to pieces before her eyes like a rotten piece of cloth. No one tear was important but all together they had succeeded in pulling it to shreds. That five minutes on the road, those minutes looking at the new Falcon, those seconds spent on the creaking hangar doors, the hour waiting for the customs man, the hour lost in the Swiss valleys—and then, on top of all that, to lose an hour going east! Oh, that was an unexpected blow. It was too much. She felt she couldn't bear it. She was ready to cry with despair.

What were they going to do? She looked out with bleak hopelessness. The monotonous sea of clouds stretched on and on behind them. The peaks were long since lost in the distant background. It had been ages, an hour or two, since they'd seen anything. They had come down, down, down—been losing altitude steadily. They would never have time to climb back all the way to those Alpine valleys. Even if they could, the fog might have covered them by now. At best it would be a crash landing on a mountain side. And ahead, just the same, an endless blanket of gray clouds, with only that slit of golden sky, that promise of another world, too far away for them to reach. What would they, what could they, do?

She was trembling again, from being keyed up. Yes, and from fear. Now, she thought, grimly, now was the time for all those noble sentiments she admired so lightly and easily when she was lying safe at home in her bed. This was the time—if there ever was one—to test them. That soldier's poem. He was a gallant man. Perhaps saying his poem would help, like an incantation, like touching the hand of a courageous person.

It was not easy. The words came out awkwardly, as though they had not proceeded from her at all, as though she had no connection with them, like words tapped out on a typewriter:

> Was it so hard, Achilles,
> So very hard to die?
> Thou knowest and I know not—
> So much the happier I.
>
> I will go back this morning
> From Imbros over the sea;
> Stand in the trench, Achilles,
> Flame-capped, and shout for me.

Eve stared at the black words as though printed on a white sheet before her. They meant nothing. They did not even seem to reach her. They were out there somewhere at arm's length. And when she tried to touch them they slipped through her fingers like smooth counters. She could not hang on to them. They did not help. No, nothing helped. She knew at last. There was no help, no help at all. This is the pit, she said to herself. I am in it. I am alone. I am abandoned. They have abandoned me. There is no one and nothing to help me. Nothing to do, except to hang on. To hang on to oneself and one's control, without hope, without reason, without feeling, without spirit, without any meaning whatsoever. Just to hang on—like a stone.

VIII

LIKE A MAPLE SEED

THE plane quivered slightly and the horizon slid around past the framework of the hatch. Eve sat up sharply. They were turning off course. Why? Where? Toward the mountains? No, away from her imaginary line of Apennines, out toward the Mediterranean—if that *were* the Mediterranean out there. Gerald was circling—over what? Nothing, as far as she could see, unless perhaps a slightly darker patch in the clouds. Could he see land below? Her heart jumped at the thought as she peered down into those shifting shadowy troughs. No—nothing. Oh, she realized, taking in her breath quickly, he meant to go down through, *blind*. My God, was it as bad as that? They had never been at this point before. Go down blind through the stuff, circle down, stall down, pancake into what? Water? Mountains? Trees? Crash before you see? Hook a wing? He said once he thought he could do it, even at night, stall down so slowly and with such control of the ship that they'd get out "without serious trouble." But he wasn't thinking about mountains. And he'd never try it unless he had to. There was nothing else to do then.

The alternatives were worse. She summed them up swiftly in her mind. Not fuel enough to climb back over the Alps into the clear air on the other side. Not time enough to land before dark in one of those open valleys on this side—even if they could still be found, even if they were still open. And as for that streak of sky ahead—they didn't dare wait for it. Suppose it weren't clear when they got there, then they'd have to do the same thing, stall down—and at night. That would be worse.

This was the last chance then. The day was gone. It would get darker every moment now. It was still light above the clouds but that was a deceptive light, she knew. It would do them no good. Once they went under the clouds it would be like going into the shadow of a house after sitting out in the glow of a fading sunset; suddenly it would be dark. This was dead serious. They'd never been in anything as bad before—worse than that time in the August mists over the Faeroe Islands, or in the November fog in Holland, or that autumn storm in the south of France. Never before had they lost ground contact without radio, without another engine, without word of a clear port ahead, without time, without light, without fuel. This was the end; this was it.

No, she couldn't say poetry or philosophize or even be afraid. There was not time. All fear dropped off her, all despair. This was a time for action. She started to clean up her cockpit in a fever of activity. It was like the fever of activity which attacks a mother whose labor pains have started. If she has other children, she is not afraid. All fear goes. Something lies ahead of her that is bigger than life. But before she can reach it,

the little odds and ends of life must be attended to first
—all unfinished work for the other children, the house-
hold. Everything must be left in order. Very soon now
she will have to neglect them, her house, her charges,
all those in her home for whom she is responsible.
Just a few minutes remain to spend on them. Quick
now, that button on sister's dress. Put away the laun-
dry. Tidy up the toy-chest. See there's food in the
house. Leave a note for the milkman about that extra
quart. She works at top speed and with a kind of joy
in the work itself, a last act of love which will stretch
on after she has gone.

So Eve worked now, with a kind of satisfaction in
doing work preparatory to a great test. She put away
her map. She turned around to see that the bundles
in the baggage compartment were fastened down
tightly. She felt along the control wires that led back
beside her feet, to make sure no handkerchief was
caught there. Everything must be in clean working
order. The extra stick was firmly snapped into its
bracket where she would not knock it accidentally with
her knee. She wiped off the windshield carefully. A blur
of grease might cut down vision at just the vital spot.
She might see ground before he did and be able to
warn him. Rescue the belt-buckle which had fallen to
the floor. Take off her dark glasses. Fragments of flying
glass wouldn't help any. There now, all was in order.
She snapped on her safety belt and sat ready, alert,
watching the front cockpit, waiting for word from her
husband. There might be something else she could do.

Gerald raised himself in the cockpit, his big shoulders hunching up in the brown leather coat. He pulled down the sides of the hatch to get his head out in the open. There was nothing between him now and the weather. He could see his enemy clearly. He tightened his belt. He pulled down his goggles. Eve felt he was putting on armor for the fight. She went through every motion with him. That's right, she was saying to herself, buckle on the armor. Get every advantage—you need it.

He turned back for an instant and shouted tersely—"Got your belt on?" She nodded. She knew what his words meant: Be prepared for anything. I will—I am, she wanted to answer back. She longed to tell him so, to squeeze his hand, to touch him. But she knew she must not. It might weaken the armor. One had to have armor in times like this. One had to have weapons. And the weapons must be clean. The blade must not be dulled by ephemeral emotions. The blade itself had been forged by emotion, compacted and fired to hard metal by deep emotion now forgotten. Emotion had turned to steel. Besides, it wasn't necessary to touch him. He knew, anyway, she was certain. Right through the hard steel insulation of his not-knowing, he knew what she was feeling. Unconsciously they were to-gether, part of the same thing at this moment. What would it be—death? Eve wondered with a curious objectivity. Very likely, she reflected coolly. They'd never been so near it before.

What were the chances? She weighed them gravely in the cold and brilliant light of this emergency. Never had her mind been so clear. Never had it worked bet-ter. All the mists of fear, dreams, and self-deception had been burnt clean by the blinding flash of realization of what faced them. Under this light she could see the minutest objects clearly, like the vision of super-reality that opens up in the crack of lightning from a midnight storm. (Never, one thinks, gazing out of the nursery window for that dazzling half second, was the garden so vivid. Each tree, each flower stands up alive, vibrant and alone. One can even see the little painted cups the children have been playing with in the sand-box, left out overnight, standing all tipsy in the drenched and printed sand, and half filled up with rain.)

What then were the chances of their getting out? Eve weighed them carefully, with steady hands, putting the arguments on the scales in her mind. Yes, there was a chance of escape. There was a chance there would be a ceiling. They might be over sea, or fields, or in a valley. There was a chance they would see enough—in time enough—to pull out, anyway to make some kind of a landing. And on the other side? (For there were chances against them, too.) There was the chance of the plane getting out of control, "falling off" as he tried to stall it down—the chance of it going into a spin. She didn't think that would happen. Gerald was too good a pilot. No, they were much more likely just to hook a wing in the side of a hidden mountain. A sound of cracking—impact—and it would all be over.

Yes, death was down there. A tremor went through her as she said the word to herself, as she looked it in the eyes. But it was not a tremor of fear. There was not a trace of fear left in her. Why not? Was she not the

timid, the doubting, the imaginative, the un-gallant?
She ought to be afraid, but she was not. Where was
fear? It was not there. It was as if she had never known
the word, *fear,* what it was. Although she had been
driven by fear for the last hour or two, it was now a
strange sensation she had forgotten, discarded, dropped
behind there in the room she had just left. She had
taken it off as one takes off an outer coat in the waiting
room of a doctor's office. She had been afraid in the
waiting room, but here, no. It was only the anteroom
of death, then, that was so terrible, she realized in a
flash of perception. It was not the room of death itself, not when you opened that inner door and stood
in the holy of holies. It was only the anteroom that was
so terrible. And they had left the anteroom.

They were turning slowly, sinking gently toward
this cushion of clouds. Gerald pulled back the throttle.
The motor eased to a sigh. The flaps went out with a
slight jolt. She could feel the plane quiver. It seemed
to stop in mid-air when those flying brakes went on,
as if they had hit another medium. Not air, something
denser, like water, or even more glutinous, like mo-
lasses.

Now they were diving into the well of the cloud,
head down into the white cotton wool. The first wisps
over the wings. The quiver as they went under. Now
there was no turning back. They were in it. They must
go through it. Nothing to do but wait, sinking down
into the mist darkly. For it was dark here. The mist
covered them up, closed over their heads, shut out the
sky, beaded the cockpit covers with tiny runnels of

rain. Was there no ripple left on top to show where they went under? No bubbles rising to the surface like the bubbles rising from a sinking ship or a drowning man? For they were submerged now, wheeling, turning, floating, like a leaf on a gentle current of air; like a maple seed poised on the certainty of a shaft of air, drifting, turning, falling to earth on a still autumn day —softly falling to death.

There was so much time; it was so quiet. The engine, throttled down, made almost no vibration, no noise. The sound of the motor was like deep sleep-breathing. She was not afraid; she was not sorry for herself. There was no time for fear, for self-pity. Time? Yes, there was time, all the time in the world. But there was no space, no room in her heart for anything but this new and overpowering sensation which filled her to the brim. What was it? Not resignation (There was nothing stoic about it.); not joy (For surely death was waiting down there.). No, it was a kind of positive acceptance and she reposed on it in complete peace and calm, like the maple seed on the shaft of air.

It gave her a sudden sense of luxury—all this peace and calm. Now, at last, she felt, all those petty details of life were attended to. Now, at last, I can turn to the big thing before me. Now I can sink down into myself and uncover the secret, the beautiful secret, that is waiting for me at the bottom of my heart. What is it? Oh, what is it?

Only once before could she remember having this sense of a secret, deep within her, waiting to be uncovered. It was when she was very ill after Peter's birth,

so ill and weak in the hospital that she was not yet back
to earth, still unattached, floating somewhere in another realm. She remembered plainly one night when
they were fussing over her, tumbling her around in
bed, eternally washing and dressing, attending to the
last evening routine, how she felt she could bear it no
longer. If only they would leave me alone, she had
thought in an anguish of mental—not physical—impa-
tience. If only the nurse would get finished with all
these unimportant details and leave me alone. There
is something within me waiting for me—(With painful
expectation she yearned toward it.)—something beautiful but I do not know what it is. And finally, when the
white uniform said "good night" and clicked the door
shut, she had turned with a flood of relief. Trembling
with anticipatory joy, she turned away from earth; she
sank down within herself to find the secret. And what
was it—this secret, this utterly beautiful thing hidden
in her heart? It was simply, as far as she could make
out, the thought of Gerald. Not Gerald as a husband,
as the father of her child. Not Gerald as a companion.
She could not see his face or touch his hand. It was no
fleshly Gerald, no Gerald that had any connection with
her, or her new child, or their relationship. She was
too far removed from earth and life to feel that. It was
the essence of Gerald, all alone, without her, in the
world. Gerald existed. A man like that existed. He
lived. God had made him. And she was full of joy
merely at the thought of his existence, as one can feel
joy at the memory of a Greek temple once seen all
alone on a green hillside. One can feel joy at remem-

bering its white flower-like perfection without wishing
to own it or be in it. One can feel joy even though one
knows one may never see it again.

And now, spiraling to death, freed from the anx-
ieties of life, what was it that waited again for her
discovery? What was this beautiful gift at the bottom
of her heart? It was again, perhaps, Gerald. She was
full of a strange ecstasy and when she attempted to put
this ecstasy into words, they came out with difficulty,
in little simple phrases, in driblets, like water hopping
from a narrow-necked bottle. We are together, she
said. I am glad we are together. I do not mind dying.
I am glad for our life. It has been a wonderful life. It
has been short, only ten years—but still, we have lived
more in those ten years than most people in their whole
lives.

Peter—yes—she was sad about Peter. Peter needed
her. That was pain. (You might have let me live a
little longer for him, God; he needs me.) But it was
numb pain, like pain under morphine, real, but a long
way off. She had wanted to teach Peter, to show him
so much; how to meet life, how not to be afraid of the
hard things in life—the fears, the doubts, the good-
byes. But perhaps—the thought fell into place easily
and simply in her mind, like the resolution of a chord
in music—perhaps their death would teach him more.
Perhaps her death would teach him, show him, what
she never could in life—not to be afraid. To take life
in both arms—like this, yes. For was this not what she
was doing?

Deeper, deeper into the clouds they sank, but so

gently. No sound, no sight, no quiver to disturb this soft descent into the underworld. She never thought that meeting death would be so gentle. And deeper, deeper into herself she sank. For there was something else down there, gleaming at the bottom of the pool— some precious stone she had not yet managed to touch, in the shadowy depths, below Peter, below Gerald. What was it, then?

Just *life,* she realized slowly, as the jewel tempted her on and its light spread, glowing under water, until it filled all her heart. This then was life:—not to be hurried, not to be afraid, not to be imprisoned in oneself. To be open, aware, vulnerable—even to fear, even to pain, even to death. Then only did one feel ecstasy filling one up to the brim. Then only did one know what life was. Then only did one taste it, drink of it, drown in it. This then was life, this full, rich and timeless last second before death.

Seconds? Surely not seconds. She smiled at the human language which insisted on cutting up the great bolt of unbroken satin into snippets of samples. She was no longer boxed up in time. She had broken through the shell again. She had cracked the husk of time. And the seed that fell out—what had this to do with time? What had this to do with time—this great oak which burst from the fallen seed? What had this to do with time—this boundless ocean into which she broke, this unlimited sky to which she soared? This song she was about to sing, to pour forth her heart upon, this wave of song. Just now—oh, why *now,* just now, at the end of her life?

This only, this slender thread of regret, held her to life. Why had she learned so late? A spider's thread, it was, but it held her. For, somehow, while accepting, sinking into this feather-like descent, she was still watching too. Every instant and with every ounce of concentration in her, she was watching the turn of the low wing for what it would show—death or escape. It did not occur to her not to watch, to sit back and close her eyes and accept in faith whatever it might be. That was a denial of life; she could not do it. She had to keep her eye fastened on that low wing, cutting like a scythe softly through layers of mist. But before she could see anything off its knife-like edge, she was numbly aware of a slight movement in front of her. Out of the side of her eye she could see—read, feel almost, for she did not dare take her glance off the wing-tip—her husband's head moving up and down. She still kept her eye doggedly on the wing. Then, again, that same motion. His head was moving up and down; he was nodding, with assurance—yes, with relief.

At last, she let go her watch; she turned; she looked at him. Yes, she was not mistaken; his head was moving up and down determinedly. It was speaking to her, as vividly as the gesture of a hand, as the sound of his voice. It said, "Yes—yes, it's all right, then. What I thought—what I hoped—a ceiling!" She read all that in his slow pronounced nod.

Her glance shot back quickly to the wing and she saw what had made him nod. First it was only a slightly different texture to the mist as though it were feathered. Oh, it was water—waves—the sea! Then, abruptly, the coast on their left, steep volcanic hills, green and tropical, dotted with towns ("the hill towns of Italy"). The engine picked up again, roared out in confidence. The plane took a leap forward. Now they could see, now they could go ahead. Vibrations sang through the ship as though a heart had started beating again. It was suddenly warm and damp. They could smell the earth beneath them, fresh with rain. And see it, too, in the subdued light. For there was no brightness here, no late afternoon glow as there had been on the tops of the clouds. They had sunk to dusk. An underwater world it was, but solid and real.

Above them was that gray curtain they had just come through, dark, overhanging, right down on the hilltops, a lid on the world. Not a break anywhere, not a trace of the gray twilit ice-flows above. The world had been sliced in half by this cloud layer, evenly and neatly at a precise water level. The mountains rose and disappeared in the mist at exactly the same point everywhere. These were the knees of the giants whose heads they had played among. But you could not see above the knees. They were cut off by fog. No ceiling there— not an inch. If they'd come down there, over the hills, just a few hundred yards east, they'd have plowed right in—not a chance. Eve gave an involuntary twitch of her shoulders. It was thick, that stuff. Wonder what made him choose just this spot here, just off shore. Was it simply his luck? Or was it some sixth sense, some fine intuition that told him this particular cloud bank was different from the others—not so thick? And even here, there was a volcanic island just ahead. Its peak, too, disappeared in clouds. Suppose—

But Eve put it out of her mind with a rush of relief. It did not matter, now they were down, part of this earth again, alive, warm, breathing. Part of the world covered with little towns, houses and ports and ships, docks and railroad lines. She wanted to put out her arms to them to welcome them back like lost children. She wanted to hold all earth in her arms, so tangible, so precious, so beautiful it seemed. Had she ever noticed its beauty before? Was it beauty? That was the wrong word for this light which seemed to burn even about things that were not beautiful. For not only the green hills, the white houses, the red roofs, the gray waves, and the fields glowed and shimmered as if transfigured with an inner light. Even the smokestacks and the gas stations were lit with an intensity, a living fire. They burned, it seemed to Eve, with the touch of man and because of that touch, became precious.

Gerald turned back at her now and smiled (that long-awaited moment). "After all my promises!" he shouted back at her, pleading forgiveness. But she had no "I-told-you-so" blame left in her. She could only pat his back for choosing just that spot in the clouds, for finding his way through the stuff, for keeping his head, for his faith, his nerve—yes, for his gallantry. And simply for the joy of being with him, being alive, being reborn to earth.

For surely she was reborn to the earth. Earth rushed back at her through all her senses, tingling. She could smell it, feel it, see it, breathe it. It poured into her on every side. It fed her hunger like bread; it filled her thirst like water; it comforted her like the firm strength of a shoulder under her head. She felt like Lazarus, raised from the dead. I was blind, and now I can see. I was deaf, and now I can hear. I was numb, and now I can feel. I was dead, and now I am alive.

IX

THIS THEN WAS LIFE

SUDDENLY she was crying, sobbing violently and she could not seem to stop. The sobs shook her body until she remembered that she must not shake like that because of the child in her. For the first time since they had gone into their subterranean world she thought of the child. For the first time perhaps ever in her life she thought of the child as distinct from herself as a pregnant woman. How strange that never before had she thought of that other being, always simply of herself: "The pregnant woman." Dreadful phrase. She had always hated it. How it cheapened life, and she hated anything that cheapened life. She understood now for the first time what was wrong with the phrase. It left out the child. Of course. Why had she not seen that before? It forgot the most important thing. For it was the child that mattered—not the woman. The Bible said it better, "Mary, great with child." That was it—great with life.

For the child would now live. How wonderful. She felt full of joy at such a miracle. Because she was saved, the child would live. Or perhaps—it came to her with a sense of tremendous ice blocks cracking in her mind in the rush of warm spring waters—perhaps it was the other way around. Perhaps because of the child she was saved. She was spared in order that the child should live. She was living for that other being. One did not live for oneself; one lived for another. The mother lived for the child. She was living then for the child which, she somehow felt, had been given to her for the first time.

For in this swift release from death, this rebirth to life, she felt that the child had been given to her anew. She was fully conscious of the gift as though it had been put into her arms. But why? For what purpose? Why was she entrusted with this gift? It overwhelmed her. What a gift—what a trust—this gift of a child, of life. Was she worthy of such a gift?

She put her hand inside her flying suit over the warm curve of her body. She took a deep breath, two or three. Now she was calm, quiet, her body relaxed. Now she could feel the child. In the intense and secret peace of that moment she could feel it move, stir gently against her side. It was strange, such a little stir, so slight, like the gentlest ripple of wind across a field of grass. But it seemed to her like a stir in the earth, like the turn of a season; as the wind across the field of grass may mean the turn of the season. The world turned in her, ever so gently. Life turned, life moved. This then was life. This—my God—life! And she was aware suddenly of the immensity of that force turning in her and in the world.

She was aware of that life which had been given back to her, that force in which she was permitted to share again. For the gift of life, she realized, was not just the clod crumbling under the foot. It was not the last red berries on the bush. It was greater than all this. Greater than her or Gerald or Peter, waving out of his window at home, or this new child curled up in her like an April fern. It resided in her for an instant—and in the clod and in the red berries—but it was not hers. It did not belong to her. It was apart from her, separate, *other* than her. That was the miracle of life which she now understood for the first time. The miracle of life was in its *otherness*. The *otherness* of the wind over a field of grass; the *otherness* that a woman felt when a child stirred in her; the *otherness* she had felt filling up her heart in the descent to death. When a thing was apart from you, other than you, it was something from the outside, something that came as a gift; but not a gift to be greedily hoarded unto oneself, a gift to be held—in trust. It was given like the talents to the three servants in the Bible story. She had never quite understood that parable. Why was he treated so badly, that third servant, the poor unprofitable servant who hid his talent in the earth? He was only cautious and a little unenterprising. Why was he banished to outer darkness? She understood it now. He had treated the money as his own and he had hoarded it. " 'I was afraid,' " said the unprofitable servant, " 'and hid thy talent in the earth.' " No, you were not to be afraid. You were not to hoard your gift, to clutch at it, to bury it in the ground, for then it was taken away.

And what had she done all her life but hoard her great gift? For she had always realized its value. She had been, in fact, oppressed by its value. But she had thought of life as a possession, as something to be hoarded and so she had judged its value falsely. It was precious, she thought, because it was threatened. Threatened by loss (the good-byes which circumvented it on every side); threatened by danger (by long flights, by war); threatened simply by the urgency of time passing (the hound of time which snapped at her heels). Threatened by separation, and danger and time (time, which is only another kind of fear).

But in the slow spiral through the shrouded clouds, as in the swift one over her home at the beginning of their trip, she had discovered the true essence of life. Not because she was hanging on to it more tenaciously in those instants; not because of the proximity of separation and death; not because, as she had once thought, "the meat is sweetest close to the bone—" but because in both cases she had let go of life, because the claws of fear had ceased to clutch at her. All those fears which come from looking on life as a possession had at last left her.

And so, life was given back to her. It was all around her. It was in Gerald's brown grease-stained coat. It was in her tired body, stiff with cold and weariness. It was in the valleys below them, in the fields wet and pungent with rain, and in the towns too; in the ugliness and in the beauty; in the flowering trees and in the railroad tracks; in the gas stations and the smokestacks; in all that was now being covered up by the dark; and in the tiny lights twinkling on through that darkness. It was in the airport they were approaching; in the men who would soon help them roll the plane into the hangar—men who shared with them the gift of life. It would be in the first feel of earth to her foot, cold and tingling as it hit the ground; in the cup of bitter coffee they would drink at the airport—yes, and in the crisp crust of bread and the rind of cheese, into which she would sink her teeth.

But especially life was in her, in the child. It was more vivid as a symbol in the child. Perhaps because she had learned through the child, the renewal of the child in her, that life was a gift, yes, but not a possession. It was given in trust—like a child. One was dedicated to it but one could not own it. Like that white temple all alone on a green hill, one could guard it, one could give to it, one could serve it, one could love it. One could—above all—like the psalmist, sing it hymns of praise.